The
Braid
Girls

The
Braid
Girls

Sherri Winston

LITTLE, BROWN AND COMPANY
New York   Boston

Little, Brown and Company
Hachette Book Group
1290 Avenue of the Americas, New York, NY 10104
Visit us at LBYR.com

First Edition: June 2023

Little, Brown and Company is a division of Hachette Book Group, Inc. The Little, Brown name and logo are trademarks of Hachette Book Group, Inc.

The publisher is not responsible for websites (or their content) that are not owned by the publisher.

Little, Brown and Company books may be purchased in bulk for business, educational, or promotional use. For information, please contact your local bookseller or the Hachette Book Group Special Markets Department at special.markets@hbgusa.com.

Library of Congress Cataloging-in-Publication Data
Names: Winston, Sherri, author.
Title: The braid girls / Sherri Winston.
Description: First edition. | New York : Little, Brown and Company, 2023. | Audience: Ages 8–12. | Summary: "Three girls start a hair-braiding business at their summer camp to make money, while competing against a rival business that threatens their plans." —Provided by publisher.
Identifiers: LCCN 2022057176 | ISBN 9780316461597 (paperback) | ISBN 9780316461610 (hardcover) | ISBN 9780316461603 (ebook)
Subjects: CYAC: Camps—Fiction. | Hair—Fiction. | Moneymaking projects—Fiction. | African Americans—Fiction. | Racially mixed people—Fiction. | Friendship—Fiction.
Classification: LCC PZ7.W7536 Br 2023 | DDC [Fic]—dc23
LC record available at https://lccn.loc.gov/2022057176

ISBNs: 978-0-316-46161-0 (hardcover), 978-0-316-46159-7 (pbk.), 978-0-316-46160-3 (ebook)

Printed in the United States of America

LSC-C

Printing 1, 2023

I want to dedicate this book to
my sister Janice Marie Winston.
A girl couldn't have a better hype man.
LOL. I love you for your continued faith
in me. It matters and so do you.

CHAPTER 1

Daija

My stapler drills into the corkboard. With each *bap-bap-bap*, pink sheets of paper flutter. So do my nerves.

We're papering the area with flyers for our business. Mine and Maggie's. We need our plan to work. Like, I really, *really* need it. But I'm trying not to "get ahead of myself," as my mom, Kiki, might say.

Gym shoes squeak across the polished community center floor; kids' voices echo off the walls. I step back from the board and take a look, hands on my hips.

This looks good. Feels good, too. It is official.

"Girl, we're gonna be a hit!" I say, using my best fake-it-till-you-make-it grin. I'm with my girl, Maggie. She hits me with the arched brow.

"You really think so?"

"I know so. The Braid Girls are jumping off in a big way! And our plan is unstoppable," I say. I sling an arm over her shoulders and squeeze.

"If you say so," Maggie says. That girl wears uncertainty like lip gloss, only her doubts keep her from shining. Me? I'm all about the shine.

I make a face, twisting my lips around while I make my eyes pop. Pretty soon we're laughing.

We're going to make beaucoup money braiding hair all around Tangerine Bay! I love hooking my girls up with hairdos that are killin' the game almost as much as I love flexing my ballet skills.

Take a bow. Applause. Applause. I know. I'm a star. Ciseaux. Ciseaux. Ciseaux. I leap in my best version of the scissor-kick leap, landing and twirling in a perfect pirouette.

Now both of Maggie's uncertain brows are high.

"This is a twirl-free zone," she says, giving me a side eye. "You know how your one-woman show frightens me." She's so not frightened.

"*Shut up!*" I laugh. "And stop chewing that thumb-nail like it's deep fried and covered in hot sauce." Then we're both laughing again.

Rising as high on my toes as I can, I extend my arms. I can't go en pointe yet in ballet, but I'm getting there. Which is why I need us—me and Maggie—to earn money this summer.

Paying for extra ballet classes is no joke! *You feel me?*

And I need the extra help. Dance is everything to me. Maggie, she's really smart. She's good at math. Someday she'll probably go to business school and head a corporation and be a bazillionaire and start a company like TikTok or something.

Me? I'm just trying to make it out of middle school without failing. And I...I need to make my father recognize how important ballet is to me, even if Kiki refuses to let me ask him to pay for anything.

"He doesn't need us," Kiki said after they split up, "and we don't need him." She told me if he offered something, that was fine, but I shouldn't ask for his help. Kiki always goes on and on about how she wouldn't have us relying on him.

And since pride don't pay the bills, me and Kiki get by on what she earns as an acting coach and drama teacher in the high school theatre department. Not starving by any means, but sometimes... money gets tight!

Maggie, switching from her usual soft-spoken ways, turns on her calculator brain and drops some real knowledge:

"We'll need to do at least ten heads a week, charging forty dollars per style for more complicated styles, plus twenty-five dollars a head for upkeep styles and general styling per person, for a total of six hundred fifty dollars. Divided by two, that's three hundred and twenty-five dollars each. I did the math."

My mouth drops open. Of course she did the math.

Maggie may *want* to earn money for the summer, but she doesn't *need* it—not like I do.

So, when Maggie came up with the idea of taking our braiding skills to the streets, I knew I had to make it happen. I might not be as good with math as Maggie, but my formula is simple:

1. Earn money to pay for extra ballet lessons.
2. Get a lead role in the fall showcase.
3. Show my father that I'm not some little kid playing around, that I'm serious—and I *am* serious!

Bap! Bap! Bap-bap-bap!

Maggie is a crafter, and homegirl knows how to work some hair. I am good at braiding, but with Maggie, it's art. I have to give her props for that.

"When is the audition for your fall showcase?" Maggie asks.

Audition.

Just the word makes my stomach twist. Sort of in a good way—the way that leaves me breathless knowing that if I get a lead role, it'll be because I've earned it. Sort of in a not-so-good way—like, what if I take the extra lessons and still don't get a lead in the show? What if I don't get any role?

My father is all about being determined, committed, and hardworking.

I miss him so much. He and Kiki broke up when I was six. It was hard on me then; it still is. But there's no time for whining when you could be grinding. Getting a big role and showing how much I have improved as a dancer—my father would have to appreciate that. Respect it.

"Auditions are the last weekend of July; the show is September twenty-ninth, I think." I step onto a bench, trying to sound nonchalant. Playing it cool, you know? I hope Maggie doesn't notice my knees trembling as I place our flyer above some others.

"The end of September? *Sweet!* That's when my braces come off! Um, do you really want to put the poster so high? Might be hard for people to see our emails? Well, maybe it's all right. I dunno. What do you think?"

I sigh. Maggie is creative and smart, but baby girl can't make up her mind, sometimes. She makes statements that sound like questions. Still, when I take a second look at the flyer, I know she's right—it's too high to read. I remove the flyer, climb down, and restaple it.

"Daija," she says, "what's the deal with the showcase?"

I pause and look over at her. "You mean, like, what is it?"

"Yes," she says, nodding.

"Miss March, one of the ballet instructors at my studio, is doing the choreography. She only chooses the best of the best because the girls from our dance school will be performing alongside professionals from the local ballet company. And she won't even consider anyone from the studio who can't go en pointe. I want one of those roles!" *Desperately!*

"That doesn't give you a lot of time," Maggie says, worry on her face. We collect the pile of flyers and head to another board. "I mean, it's already June."

"I know, Maggie. You just wait," I say, furiously stapling my frustrations into the flyers. *Bap! Bap! Bap!* "As long as we can keep earning money from braiding, I'll be able to pay for those extra classes. And that will get me through."

"And I will have launched my first real business!" says Maggie, grinning. "With the help of my best friend and business partner. I just want us to enjoy ourselves, make some money, and do, you know, friendship stuff."

Bap! Bap! Bap!

I staple another flyer while standing on a step-stool. I look down at Maggie and say, "You mean like make friendship bracelets and write 'BFFs' on our notebooks?"

She looks up and swipes playfully.

"There's nothing wrong with friendship bracelets," she says.

I laugh. "Yeah, yeah, I know." She smiles and I smile back. Going into seventh grade in the fall will be a lot easier with a friend like her around.

People at school always ask if we're sisters, me and Maggie. We share the same beautiful deep-dark skin. We both have thick, long hair—I braid hers; she braids mine.

Since she moved here two years ago, we've become best friends. We're sisters, or the closest I will ever get, according to Kiki. Which makes the news she delivered back in May painful—to me at least.

"What are you thinking about?" Maggie asks, drawing my thoughts back to the here and now.

"She still coming next month?" I ask. Maggie knows who I mean. She looks down and chews the corner of her lip.

"Yep, Callie's still coming," she says. "She'll be here the middle of July, I think. She's staying with us for two weeks, then she goes to her aunt's, who lives near us in downtown Jacksonville. Daddy says she'll probably stay full-time during the week with her Aunt Lana and stay with us weekends. Until we all get used to each other, that is. Then"—she shrugs—"we'll see."

I nod, hopping down from the stepstool.

"If the girl is sus, I'll figure it out," I say as we find another location. "Trust me!"

She laughs. "You're already suspicious of her, and we haven't even met her yet."

"You have to be cautious, Maggie. That's why you need me. Protection. And I'm here for you, girl.

Besides, what kind of friend would I be if I didn't look out for you?"

Maggie smiles. "I think we're safe."

We go back to stapling as many surfaces as possible with our flyers. Maggie looks back at me and grins.

"I'm really excited about starting our business," she says. "Mom says it'll help me get used to dealing with people, make me, you know, not so...so..."

"Shy?" I say, my face looking like a big ol' "duh" sign.

My girl Maggie has great ideas, but always talks herself out of a good thing. That's what I am here for, to push her. The two of us make a great team.

That is why I feel nervous about this new sister showing up. Will having a *real* sister—even a half sister—change what me and Maggie have?

Truth is, I was pretty lonely before Maggie arrived. I missed living down in Miami. Missed my old neighborhood and friends.

And I missed my dad.

But when we met, the two of us just clicked, and it's been Daija and Maggie ever since.

Maggie is what my mom calls a pie-in-the-sky type of girl. Like, she loves thinking of ideas and imagining all the possibilities.

But me? I am the kinda girl who believes in getting it done!

We finally finish with the flyers. Passing the community pool, we see that it's filling up with kids.

"Maybe we should grab our suits. I have ballet this afternoon, but if it's cool with your folks, we could come back after. It'd be nice to work out the kinks in my muscles after my ballet workout. *Ooh!* We could go to my house and wash our hair. I'll re-braid yours if you can re-braid mine," I say.

Right then, we both hear the tinkling bell tone from Mag's phone. She looks at the screen and frowns.

"It's Daddy," she says. "He wants me to come home. He's taking us out to lunch?"

We both pull a face. Now, with me and my mom, we do things on the fly all the time. Not Maggie's folks, though.

Everybody knows the Wests are all about their routines. Fridays are not going-out-to-eat days, especially not in the afternoon.

We start toward her house when she asks, "Have you spoken with your dad lately?"

About that...

I have something to tell her that I've been putting off. Maggie isn't my dad's biggest fan. Probably because I complain to her about him when I'm feeling down. I love my dad, I really do. But sometimes... sometimes, I wish he had more time for me.

Ever since he remarried and had sons, things with us have been so *different*. Especially since me and Kiki left Miami and moved up here outside of Jacksonville.

"As a matter of fact, I have spoken with him. Um, he and my stepmom and my two little brothers are moving up here. From Miami," I say in a rush.

Talking about my dad with Maggie weirds me out sometimes, for real. Her and her dad are super close. Practically a Disney movie.

I'm not jealous. Matter of fact, I love that they are so close. Gives me hope, you know. Like maybe me and my dad can get there, too.

"Really?" Maggie says. She's got this tone, like she's suspicious. Can't blame her. When he called me, I sounded the same. Then she asks, "How do you feel about that?"

"Excited!" I say. *Dang!* That sounds so extra, even I don't believe me. "I mean, I'll see him more. So, yeah, I'm excited."

Maggie stops walking. I am a few steps ahead before I realize it. I turn.

"Are you sure?" she says, arms crossed tight. She looks away, digging the toe of one shoe in the dirt.

I put my hands on my hips and say, "What is that supposed to mean?"

Maggie shifts from foot to foot before looking at me.

"You know. Your father isn't—hasn't always been reliable. He should treat you better. I just don't want you to get your hopes up and get hurt?"

"I'm fine," I say, sighing. We're both silent for a few minutes as we walk faster.

Maggie says, "I'm glad he's moving here if it means you'll get to spend more time with him. It's a good thing." She stops again for a second and looks at me. "A really good thing. So, why the move?"

"It's a work thing," I say, wishing I could say, *Oh,*

Daddy didn't want to be so far away from his oldest child and he misses me so much that he's moving his entire family to be closer to me.

"Don't worry about it. Mags, I'm sure we'll be fine. We may not have the kind of relationship you have with your dad, but he loves me. I know he does."

Maggie's silence lingers as we pass the house of one of our known enemies in the neighborhood—Angela Cook. A little witch who picks on kids like Maggie—kids who won't fight back.

"Wonder what Angela's doing for the summer?" I ask in a devilish tone. I slide a glance at Maggie. She does an exaggerated shiver.

"Knowing her, she'll probably be somewhere terrorizing small children or giving the evil eye to helpless puppies," she says. We both laugh, and I feel a little of the tension evaporate.

At Maggie's house, we see her mom and dad standing in the yard.

Her little brother, Taz, rides his bike up and down the driveway, zigging and zagging. He whizzes down the drive and blows kisses at me, then pedals off in a flurry of mad giggles.

"Mom!" Maggie says, sounding like she is seven, same as Taz. "Please get your boy child under control."

Her parents walk to the end of the drive. Her dad throws an arm around her shoulders; she hip checks him.

I bet Mr. West doesn't blow off Maggie's dreams the way my father does my hope of becoming a professional ballerina.

Last year, when I invited him to my recital, he surprised me by actually coming. I'd been nervous. So nervous, in fact, that I made all sorts of mistakes in the dance. It was humiliating. I knew what was up. He was thinking I was no better than back in the day when he took me to my first lessons. Now we see each other so irregularly, he must still think of me as that same little kid.

"Hey, COB," Maggie's dad says, giving her a peck on the cheek. "I see you're with my Skipper."

My father is very formal. We never use nicknames. Mr. West has always called me Skipper.

"Can Daija come to lunch with us? Please, please, please?" Maggie says, prayer hands and everything.

"Yeah, can Daija come, too?" adds Taz, whizzing

past. That little stinker gives me a wink. He always makes me laugh.

Mr. West looks down at Maggie, then me.

"I'm afraid not, Skipper," he says, giving me an apologetic smile before turning back to Maggie. "COB, we've got some family things to talk through. But I promise we'll take all you girls out next week."

My bike is parked at the side of the driveway. I walk over and push it to the end of the drive. "That's okay, Mr. West, I have to get ready for my ballet workout, anyway," I say.

It is only after I've ridden halfway down the road that it sinks in.

We'll take all you girls out next week....

Not both.

All.

Looking over my shoulder, I see Maggie's face. That one eyebrow up. The slight frown. And there it is—the same question that just hit me:

What "all you girls" is he talking about?

CHAPTER 2

Maggie

The Cheesecake Factory is my favorite restaurant. I love this place, which is why I'm suspicious. It's like Daija's untrusting nature is rubbing off on me. But I'm not paranoid. Okay, I'm a little paranoid. But you've heard the old saying:

Just because you're paranoid, doesn't mean they're not out to get you!

"Mom," I say, "why are we here? *Really?*" I can feel my eyebrows rising. I may not speak up all the time, but my eyebrows are very talkative.

She doesn't miss a beat. She matches my skepticism with cheery second-grade-teacher optimism, saying, "For lunch, sweetheart."

"A likely story," I mumble.

"Put that eyebrow away, dear, and try to enjoy your food." She meets my mumbled tone with her own super-positive chirp without even breaking a sweat. Oh, she's good!

But not that good. I mean, really? Who does she think she's fooling? This place is packed. About forty minutes to get a table. Forty minutes! And yet, Mom and Daddy are willing to wait. On a Friday afternoon. They know Friday lunches are sandwiches and salads on the patio. Eating out is almost always for dinner. Not. Lunch. So why are we here? Why?

Because something is up, that's why. I tap my foot. A nervous habit. When people lie, I get anxious.

We'll take all you girls out next week.

And what was that about?

I look over at Daddy and he's reading the menu like it's a masterpiece. Normally, we're joking around or he's telling me reason #868 why I should join the navy someday. I'm not joining the navy, but don't tell him. No need to break his heart before I have to.

"I know you two are hiding something. What is it? You have to tell me," I say, looking from one to the other.

Mom and Dad used to tell people how "delighted" they were when I learned to talk before I was two. In full sentences. Now, while sitting here with my best TV detective stare, trying to give them the stink eye and asking questions, I wonder if they're still so delighted.

"You need to relax," Mom says, her cheeriness tinged with a teensy bit of desperation. She glances at my tapping feet.

Daddy looks up, glances at Mom—something goes on between them, some secret message that dangles above my head, and they know I can't stand that. Then Daddy looks back at the menu he has been studying while we wait to be seated.

The comment Daddy made back at the house, then let drift away, replays once again in my head.

We'll take all you girls out next week.

Callie isn't due here until later next month. So,

what was he talking about? Something is definitely going on. I can't have drama. Not this summer. I'm turning twelve in a few weeks. I'm getting my braces removed in September. I'm running a business with my best friend. It's supposed to be the summer of fun!

Taz is the only one saying anything. "Blah-blah-bloop-bloop-bloop-boop," he says, speaking in alien. He locks his arms at his sides and walks stiffly in front of us. I guess on his planet, the aliens are robots. I wonder if they're drama-free robots.

"Babba-ba-dee-bee-bop," I answer him back, making my eyes bulge out as much as possible. He giggles. He's so easily amused. I guess I like the little guy. At least he's fun to play with, like the puppy I've always wanted.

Finally, we're seated. I give a quick peek around the room, making sure Angela Cook isn't here. Last thing I need with all Mom and Dad's weirdness going on would be to bump into her. I can't wait till I'm grown and she needs a job. She will not be hired by MWI—Maggie West, Inc.

The dining room is packed. The columns surrounding the room are trimmed in a thick, ropelike design. It always reminds me of braided or twisted hair. The ceilings swoop and display cherubs like in old-fashioned paintings at the museum. I think they call those "frescoes."

We've only been in Jacksonville for a few years. Mom brought me and Taz here to look for a house while Daddy finished his last eight months of active duty. I was so grateful to leave Daddy's last overseas post in Japan. Being here has been the best thing to ever happen to me, thanks to Daija. I finally feel like I belong. I wasn't popular in Japan. Now I have friends and a best friend.

And I'm starting a business! Something I've dreamed about but didn't feel confident enough to do on my own.

Shortly after we're seated, Daddy says, "COB, you good?" Captain of the Boat. Daddy is all navy, all the time. He gives me a slight frown. Uh-oh. My bouncing knee is shaking the table.

"Sorry," I say. Water stops dancing in our glasses. My knee is in park.

Why won't they just come out and tell me the bad news? I know something's up.

Still, I give my best play-along smile.

Mom and Daddy are always worrying about me. It's because of "the incident." My last year or so in school in Honshu, Japan, was a nightmare. Bullies will find any reason to make your life miserable. The taunting and pressure got to be too much. I finally couldn't take it.

Two of the bullies tried stuffing me in a locker at school. Too bad they didn't know I had a lucky eight-ball. When they pulled me to the locker, I grabbed that Magic 8 Ball with both hands and—*WHAM!* I was aiming for their bellies. But I hit literally below the belt.

It wouldn't have been so bad, except one of the boys' dads was some kind of important person, and they tried to give my dad grief over it. Daddy says he decided not to reenlist because it was time to move on.

Sometimes, though, I wonder if he left because of what happened between me and those two. I hope not.

I shake my head to chase away the memories. That's when I force myself to look around the room, get out of my funk. One of my favorite things to do when I'm out is to check out people's hairstyles.

Across the center aisle of tables, two women sit practically nose to nose. Now, you know those sisters are spilling the tea. It's all in their body language. Anyway, their hair is fierce. The one in a white long-sleeved tee has her hair piled high on her head. Her thin braids have an ombre effect, from black into coppery shades of brown.

The other woman has eight or ten super-huge braids that reach all the way down her back. Their heads are underneath a light at the table. Even from here I can see their parts are sick. So, so straight.

Then I spot a couple of little girls at a nearby table who have excellently braided hair. Jumbo braids are my specialty. I can do them fast. Daija is better with some of the smaller braids. I've taught her a lot. She's gotten really good. And she does twists really well, but my cornrows are so on point. Just saying.

I turn my head and my twists—styled by Daija—shimmy around my shoulders. The little girls look over and one says, "We like your hair."

My cheeks turn warm with a blush hidden beneath rich brown skin. "Thank you," I say, lips tucked to hide my smile and my braces. Still, a teensy-weensy one leaks out. Having your hair on point feels amazing. I love coming up with styles and getting new styles myself.

Mom and Daddy are chitchatting now, which makes me feel a little less on edge.

"Are you and Daija all set to become the premier hair braiders of Tangerine Bay?" Mom asks. Now she's the one studying her menu, even though she gets the same thing every time we come—Asian chicken wrap tacos.

I nod. "We put up some flyers today inside the Tangerine Bay Community. Tomorrow we're going to the Groveland Estates," I say.

"Maggie is going to be rich!" says Taz. "We don't use money where I'm from. We collect rocks and nuts and bolts and trade them. Bloop-bloop-bloop!"

I give him a high five. "Good job, buddy. You keep collecting those rocks and bolts!"

Mom laughs softly, studying her menu like there's going to be a quiz. She looks up finally and asks me, "Did Kiki tell you and Daija about her summer camp plans?"

Now I'm studying my menu because, hey, everyone else is doing it. I look up and shake my head.

Daddy drums his fingers lightly on top of his plastic-covered menu. "I know what I'm having," he says. Unlike me and Mom, Daddy chooses something different every time we come. He says after years of going out to sea on navy vessels, eating the same food over and over, he likes as much variety in his meals as possible.

"What're you getting, Daddy?" Taz asks, but I shush him.

"Pipe down, Robot! Mom, you were saying?" I cut in, leaning an elbow on the table. Is this it? Is this the "news" they've been sitting on?

Taz rewards me by poking out his tongue and saying something in alien bloops that does not sound friendly. I think he and his planet have just declared war.

"Taz, be polite, and you, little miss, get your elbows off the table," Mom says. Daddy snickers. Mom is fully in control. Second grade teachers are ruthless, man.

"Honey, Kiki said the community center received some big grant money this summer to use on the program, so she wants to offer you guys an opportunity to be junior counselors. You and Daija will be paid. That's even more money for your fat little bank account."

Mom and Daddy like teasing me about my bank account.

Okay, I'll admit it, I'm all about my savings. I might be mild-mannered, but I don't play with my money. Now I can have a learning experience. And earn cash, too. I'll be working on my management skills and having a good time. #Goals.

"She wants us to be counselors?" I ask. "Doing what?"

"Crafts and things," Mom says. "She knows how artsy-crafty you are. You can teach crochet, drawing, collage making—things like that. And Daija can do a 'stretching for ballet' class. Maybe more, if she's up to it."

"Seriously?" I say. *Happy dance. Happy dance. Happy dance.* I don't actually stand up and dance because, well, I'd rather drop dead than draw attention to myself like that. But I do a wicked three-second shoulder shimmy.

Mom sees the money bags dancing in my eyes

and laughs. "Calm down, Baby Oprah, don't count your millions just yet."

Instantly, I go through the financial plan I've laid out for myself and our Braid Girls business.

Daddy jumps in, saying, "Maybe I'll be able to retire altogether and let Maggie take care of us!" *Sigh.*

Mom shakes her head. "She knows her money is her own."

"Why don't you ever say that about my money?" Dad says, pretending like he's hurt.

"Bloop! BLOOP! Bloop! Boop-boop!" When we look at Taz, he's balancing a spoon on his nose. Why, why, why is my family so weird?

I release the twist I've been twirling around my finger and clear my throat. "Did I hear we are getting paid?"

"It doesn't pay a whole bunch, but every little bit helps any entrepreneur. Taz is going to robotics camp at the science center. You can ride with Daija and Kiki."

We order our food, and when it comes, we all dig in. I'm hungry, and the chicken Romano is my favorite. Still, the more Mom and Daddy keep eyeing me, the more the pasta starts to taste like paste. I want to be excited about this new opportunity. But not before I know what's *really* going on.

It takes until I'm almost done before my parents finally spill it.

"Kids, we've got some more news!" Daddy says, his voice going into full game-show-host mode. He only uses that voice when he's trying to get you to taste some disgusting vegetable at Grandma's, like brussels sprouts. Or when you get kicked in the face during your first—and last—karate class and he wants you to know everything's fine.

Or when he's being deployed.

Did Daddy reenlist? My stomach drops into my knees, which are shaking up and down, up and down.

And when Mom links her arm through his, I know we're in big trouble.

This was how the whole "Daddy has a daughter he never knew about" conversation began. My seven-year-old brother looks horrified. At the same time, Taz and I ask two very different questions:

"Are you being deployed?" I squeak.

"Are you getting divorced?" Taz blurts, tears in his big round eyes.

Divorced? Well, great. Something else to worry about. I hadn't even thought of that.

A cold sweat prickles my skin, and I take several deep swallows, trying to keep the pasta and chicken down.

"Of course we're not getting a divorce," Mom says to Taz.

Dad turns to me and shakes his head. "COB, I'm not in the navy anymore. No deployments."

"But you could have reenlisted. Did you?"

"No, baby, no!" He reaches across the table and squeezes my hand. I reach over and take Taz's little hand into mine. We hold on to each other.

"Well, due to circumstances none of us could have predicted, Callie is arriving earlier than expected. Her aunt, who was going to let her stay with her here in Jacksonville while Callie got used to us...well, she has to leave—" Dad is saying.

I interrupt. "She has to leave? Well, what's going to happen to Callie?"

"Mom and I discussed it," he says, "and we feel confident you kids can get to know each other best if Callie..."

"Moves in right away!" Mom says.

"You mean, like, permanently?" I ask, my voice a whisper.

"Permanently," Daddy says, his voice soft and sincere. "She wants to get to know us—to know you guys. With her mom...deceased, we're her family now. I want us to be a part of her life, and I want her to be part of ours."

I'm reeling, of course. I like things to go as planned. I like structure, which, I know, is sort of weird for an artistic soul, but I do.

"When does she get here?" I ask, squeezing Taz's fingers a little tighter.

Mom looks between me and Taz and says in her shiniest schoolteacher voice, "She arrives on Sunday, love. Isn't that exciting?"

We'll take all you girls out next week....

Callie is coming Sunday.

And she's never leaving!

What will Daija think?

More important, how am I supposed to feel about that?

❧ CHAPTER 3 ❧

Callie

How am I sitting here—in this kitchen, with these people? A family—my family. Only they're strangers! This is not how I'd pictured it; not how I thought it would feel.

I've been dreaming about meeting my father since forever. I used to beg Mom to tell me who he was, but she wouldn't. Not until a year ago, when she got sick.

Anger still bubbles inside me sometimes when I think, *What if she'd only told me sooner?* But I know it wouldn't have made any difference. Not for her, anyway. She still would have gotten sick. Still would've...

"It's cool having you here," says Taz, the little brother. "Only I hope you don't turn out to be the mean type of big sister, like Maggie!" He breaks into a fit of giggles. She whacks his hand with a small towel without ever turning from the stove, where she's flipping French toast. Butter sizzles in the pan.

"It's so nice to be here," I hear myself say in my chirpiest voice. Taz grins while rubbing his knuckles. "I've been waiting so long to meet you and Maggie."

My half-siblings look at me and I push the wattage of the smile past a hundred. I can't seem to stop talking.

"It feels like forever since I found out about you guys. I've been so excited to meet you! I hope one day I can take you with me to the Bahamas, too. I have so many friends back there and I know they're dying to meet you, too...."

I draw a quick breath, then plow ahead before anyone else can jump in:

"There's just a ton for us to do. Do you like pirates? We could go to the Pirates of Nassau Museum or we could go to this place where they make chocolate or—*oooh! Oooh!* We have to go to Atlantis! They have so many water rides, it's sick!"

"Baby, take a deep breath or you're going to hyperventilate," says Tina West.

Taz grins and says, "Bleep-bleep-bleep-bloop-bloop."

"Huh?" I say, the wattage dimming ever so slightly. I know I must look like some clown, but I'm so scared inside that I'm actually shaking.

"Bleep-bleep-bleep-bloop-bloop," he repeats. Then he says, "I'm from another planet so I can speak alien. I was saying you have a lot of teeth."

See, that's what happens when you're grinning like a cartoon clown—you show a lot of teeth!

His comment draws a snort from Maggie, who casually reaches over and gives her brother another towel smack. "Don't be such a gerbil, Taz," she says. I can tell her manner is shy. She won't quite make eye contact with me, not directly. But I can also tell she's paying attention to everything, and she's possibly amused. I can't tell whether "amused" is good or bad.

Once a platter of fluffy scrambled eggs, another

of French toast, a tray of bacon, and a serving dish filled with golden hash browns cover the table, we seat ourselves in their kitchen.

The room is spacious—walnut cabinets, red and brown Mexican tile, flowers spilling from terracotta pots. Mama didn't cook. Our kitchen was large and modern, with all the bells and whistles—Grandma made sure of that—but it mostly felt...I don't know. Empty.

Tina and James visited me a few times in the Bahamas—once when Mama asked them to come so she could break the news about me, then one more time before she passed away. They came to the funeral and stayed a few days to make sure I was settled, and they kept in contact with me.

They came back again to discuss what I wanted to do, and we've talked on the phone since. But they wanted to hold off on telling my siblings.

My grandma was beyond mad about Mama granting legal guardianship to the Wests. She threatened to sue. Mama said she wasn't worried about it, though. She said Grandma was being her usual controlling self.

Once I moved in with Mama Conch to finish out my school year, I never heard from Grandma again. I didn't shed any tears over it.

I'm just glad the Wests are giving me a chance. But part of me is afraid, you know? Like, what if they only did it because they felt forced to? What if the only reason they said I was welcome to come here is because, like, who says no to a dying friend? Even one you haven't seen in forever?

"I hope you like the meal, Callie," Tina is saying. "Maggie is a whiz at French toast." Maggie dips her head, and I can see her amazing, deep brown cheeks blushing.

"Everything looks fantastic, thank you," I say. We dig in, delicious smells floating around us in a sweet, buttery cloud.

Taz swivels his head, eyes scanning my face, then Maggie's. His cheeks are stuffed with loads of French toast, and syrup dribbles down his chin. He narrows his eyes, making faces at Maggie.

"Taz, stop being annoying!" she says. "Do you want your...um, sister—I mean, other sister—to see you get smacked?" Maggie quickly dips her head again, embarrassed, I guess, over not knowing what to call me.

"You've already smacked me twice with the towel, Maggie. Aliens are not afraid of big sisters," he says, smugly. "But you do know that the two of you look just alike. One darker, one lighter, but the same big heads, the same gray eyes, the same dimples, 'cept yours are deeper, Maggie. Are you really our sister, Callie? Or did they clone you?"

I know everyone else is thinking it, too. I know I am. It's so weird to see another version of yourself. Our faces are so similar, almost identical. When her gaze meets mine, I am positive she has already given it some thought, too.

"Taz," James says, "boy, don't talk with your mouth full. Everyone here is related by blood, not clone science." His gaze flicks back and forth between me and Maggie. "Am I going to need to have a talk with you later?"

Uh-oh. That sounds ominous. Taz gulps and shakes his head.

"No, sir," he mumbles. When I make eye contact with James, I expect to see anger or something, but his eyes twinkle, and I can tell he's trying to hold back laughter. I feel relieved. Taz might be a little annoying, but I already feel kind of protective of this little alien.

My brain works to sort out thoughts and feelings. I was supposed to leave Nassau for Tangerine Bay in the middle of July and spend two weeks with the West family. Auntie Lana, Mama's sister, had invited me to stay with her in Jacksonville for the summer, at least, until me and the Wests all felt comfortable with the arrangement.

However, Auntie got a chance of a lifetime, winning an award that would take her around the world. The next thing you know, my trip to the Wests was moved up and now permanent. Unless we all hate one another. Then I'll go where Auntie Lana goes.

I do not want to go to some boring boarding school. I want a family.

When I look up, I see Tina searching my face— the way her eyes probe at every inch, every expression. She has that mom thing going on. You know, like when you can feel the warmth and care pouring off her. I'm pretty good at picking up people's energy. I feel the glow from Tina's soul. Good vibes, definitely.

Determination keeps my smile at a hundred watts. She reaches over and pats my hand in an "everything will be all right" kind of way, and it's all I can do not to just lose it.

I miss Mama so, so, so much.

Mama Conch told me the best way to honor Mama would be to live by her words. I really hope Mom's spirituality has rubbed off on me. She wanted me to lead a calm, balanced, spiritual, and meaningful life. I plan to try with all my might.

Laughter across the table draws me back. Hard to believe I'm really sitting across from siblings I never knew I had. I've always wanted a sister.

Did Mom know about Maggie?

I'll bet she did. Emotions shift rapidly from painful longing to the familiar shimmer of anger. I feel my lips tighten, and suddenly it's as if she's right there and we're having our millionth fight about whatever, and I'm mad enough to start shaking.

God, Mom! How could you do this to me? How could

you keep these people a secret from me, then up and die and dump me into their laps!

"Baby, you cold?" It takes a moment for me to realize the voice is directed at me. A man's voice. I look up, and James—my father—is staring at me. His eyes are just like mine—and Maggie's. Large gray irises, tipped up at the corners. Only now his are clouded with concern. For me.

I just sit there looking at him. Maybe I'm from another planet like Taz is. Maybe I should say "bloopity-bloop-bloop."

"You looked like you were shaking," he says, gently. "Are you...okay?"

I turn into a ferocious bobblehead, nodding over and over, saying, "I'm fine, I'm fine...just fine." I have a father who is concerned about me. I've never had that before.

Tina nudges Maggie, mercifully rescuing me from death by bobblehead, saying, "Why don't you tell Callie something about yourself? You kids need to get to know one another."

"*Mom,*" Maggie groans, "don't be so weird, okay?"

Taz says, "Bloop. Bloop-bloop-bee-bop-boop!"

James laughs and shakes his head.

"Go on, Maggie. Otherwise, I'll be forced to talk for you," Tina says. "Hi, Callie, I'm Maggie's mind. I like—"

"*Mom!*" Her tone is sharp, but everyone laughs except the two of us. Then she lets out a long sigh, shaking her head. "Girl, I don't know why you'd even want to come to this house of the bizarre."

"Magnolia Marie!" says Tina.

"That's okay, Maggie, I know how it is," I say, trying to sound conspiratorial, like I'm in on some family joke.

Maggie shrugs, then says, "After we eat, I'll show you around the room we'll be sharing—at least until Daddy gets his junk out of the spare room and fixes it up for you!" She says this while looking sternly at her father.

"Okay, it's a deal," I say.

James shoos everyone away after we eat. "I've got cleanup duty. Me and my first mate. Right, Taz?"

"Aw, man!" says Taz. Then he mumbles angrily, "Bloop! Boop! Bam!" For James's sake, I hope that wasn't some sort of intergalactic battle cry.

The room Maggie leads me to is spacious. "It's a second main bedroom," she says without making eye contact. She says her room is the same size as her parents', and both open onto the back garden and patio.

It's weird being in her bedroom. A girl's room is her safe space. It's personal. I feel like an intruder. The walls are covered with photos, artwork, and a few really intricate crochet wall hangings.

I reach out and touch one. "Did you make this?" I ask.

Maggie is standing beside a stuffed sofa the color of fresh blueberries. She says, "This couch lets out to a bed. You can sleep here, okay?"

"Okay."

She takes a breath, then walks over to me and the wall hanging. Her smile appears, wide and unexpected. "Yes," she says, hands pressed in a prayer pose. "I made this a few years ago with my granny. She's the one who taught me how to braid, too."

Now we stand before each other, each of us taking a long surveying look at the other. We're the same height, both of us with long legs and athletic bodies—Maggie with more muscles than I have.

"It's weird, right?" Maggie says, shyly.

"Totally weird," I say.

"Are you as nervous as I am?" she says with a giggle.

I nod, once again turning into a bobblehead. "*Sooooo* nervous."

"Um...," Maggie begins, "I'm not always talkative, but it doesn't mean I'm mad or upset. It just means I'm quiet."

"Well, girl, I am almost never quiet, except when listening to music. And I'm trying to live life in the zen zone," I say.

She gives a sly smile and says, "Okay, here's the deal: I can't do giddy, especially not early in the mornings."

I snap a salute, and she laughs again.

"Daddy's going to clean out the spare room so you can have a room of your own, but for now, my room is your room. We have an en suite bathroom, and since the room has a double closet, I took some boxes and stuff to the garage to make space for your clothes."

Her welcoming spirit touches me so much that I

feel a tear in the corner of my eye. "Thank you" is all I manage to say.

She smiles. "I do like your braids," she says. "How long have you been braiding?"

Now we move to two beanbags and drop onto them. The door to her room flies open and Taz runs in, leaving a trail of bloops, and leaps onto her. I expect her to get mad at him and push him away, but instead, she wraps her arms around him and drops her chin on top of his head.

"Does he do that sort of thing often?" I ask, unable to stop laughing.

"Yep!" she says.

Just as quickly as he arrived, Taz dashes off again. We both laugh. I turn back to her and say, "Um, I started braiding when I was about ten. Mama Conch, my mom's good friend, was like a grandmother to me. Better than my real one, that's for sure. Anyway, she showed me how and I practiced a lot."

Maggie grins wide. "My grandma...well, I guess your grandma, too, taught me at the same age. I didn't really start doing my own hair until I was ten.

That was two years ago. Now I'm much faster—and better, if I do say so myself. My best friend, Daija, did my hair for today. You'll meet her tomorrow."

"Awesome!"

"We're, um...," Maggie's voice tapers off, and I see her shyness creep back in.

"What is it?" I ask. I reach out and touch her hand. She takes my hand and looks at my henna design.

"It's so pretty," she whispers.

"Thanks! I brought my henna stuff. I'll do one for you, if you'd like."

Maggie nods and says, "I'd like that." Then she takes a deep breath, as if deciding something. "Daija and I have a braiding business. It was my idea, but Daija is the one who actually made it work. You'll love her. She's really, really nice. A little bossy some-times, but meeting her when we moved here has changed my life."

"I can't wait to meet her," I tell her.

She takes another breath, then says, "Maybe, um...I don't know, maybe you might want to join us? You know, be part of our team. The Braid Girls."

She's giving me a questioning look, and I can feel

my cheeks growing warm. The knot that had been rolled tight in my chest since I stepped off the plane starts to ease and flatten out.

"Yes! I'd love that!" I say. Then I find the suitcase with my henna materials, dig them out, and arrange them on a low table. We talk easily, and before long, I think both of us are feeling more comfortable.

I'm going to make this work. Zen, and perfect, and calm. Maggie will see. I'm going to be the best business partner, best sister, and best friend she's ever had.

❧ CHAPTER 4 ❧

Daija

Kiki is sliding me little glances in the car, so I'm like, "Go ahead, Kiki. I can tell you've got something to say."

It's Monday morning, and we have to set up for the start of camp on Tuesday. Mom is driving to pick up Maggie. And I want to lay my eyes on the new sister! From the pictures Maggie sent, they do look alike. But I want to see her up close and in person.

I don't care how alike they look, as long as she understands that I am Maggie's best friend *and* her sister.

Kiki maneuvers our car into a right lane and turns into the Groveland Estates entrance. She lets out a big sigh and I grit my teeth for whatever drama is happening now.

After turning her head right to left and cracking a few kinks in her neck, Kiki is like, "Okay, look, your father called last night and said he can't take you to dinner this week—like he promised he would."

Then she slides a look in my direction like she is expecting me to flip out so *she* can flip out and remind me why their marriage didn't work and why I should accept that we don't need him and blah, blah, blah.

I am not trying to hear any of it.

Kiki's relationship with my father is between *them*. I want my own relationship with him. And now that he has moved to Jacksonville, I am determined to make that happen.

"He's probably still caught up with moving and everything," I say quickly. Of course, I'd been so excited about going to dinner with them—my father, his twin five-year-olds, and my stepmom. Still, I'm not going to get all weepy or whatever about it. That's not me. Even if it does hurt.

"He'll make it happen when he's not so busy." I sound confident. You know, easy-peasy.

"Hmmph!"

We ride in silence for the next two blocks until we pull into Maggie's driveway. I can feel Kiki's anger rolling off her. I snap:

"What's your problem? It's no big deal, okay?" I climb out of the car and slam the door.

"Hey, don't take it out on me because he can't do what he promises. I'm just the messenger!" She slams her door, too, and we both stomp up the drive.

Kiki and I don't have a normal mother-daughter relationship. I've always called her Kiki. Always.

She and my father were high school sweethearts in Miami. Apparently, I was her high school graduation present. *Surprise! Here's your diploma. You're going to be a mom!*

I grew up going to commercial auditions with Kiki. Sometimes she didn't want the producers or managers to know she had a kid, so I pretended to be her little sister. It wasn't as bad as it sounds. We had fun back then. Even though Kiki has had to hustle all her life, especially after her and my father split apart, she's never made me feel guilty about it.

We just bicker sometimes.

But as usual, she leans into me, bumping me in the shoulder, and says, "Sorry, kiddo. You know your father drives me up a wall! I just don't want to see you hurt."

She squeezes my cheeks and makes smoochie faces. *Ew!* Gross.

I swat at her hand. "Kiki! Cut it out!"

But we both laugh, and like usual, we're cool again.

Then Taz pulls the door open wearing a white undershirt and Spider-Man pajama bottoms. When he sees Kiki, his eyes bug out. He might have a crush on me, but his love for her is supreme.

"Hi, Miss Kiki!" he sings before dipping his eyes, as if her beauty is too much to behold. For goodness' sake! He is grinning like it's picture day. Kiki, being the big ol' flirt she is, sweeps him into her arms and starts kissing his face. His giggles fill the air.

"Where's Maggie?" I ask, pushing past the love fest.

"Everybody's out back having breakfast. We made enough for everyone. Come on, Miss Kiki, eat with me! You can have some, too, Daija!" Gee, glad I'm included.

He slides from her grasp to the ground, grabs her hand, and starts leading us through the kitchen to the back door.

Of course, Maggie and I talked last night about the whole sister situation. Maggie being Maggie, she tried to make it sound like everything was fine. But I need to meet this chick and see for myself.

We didn't expect Callie to come so early, or, as Maggie told me on FaceTime Saturday, to be staying permanently. All of a sudden, she's here a month early and ready to be part of the family. Well, I say, not so fast!

Maggie is not only shy but also naïve. It's up to me to make sure she doesn't get walked on by this girl. And I have to make sure Callie isn't going to try pushing her way between me and Maggie.

When we step onto the patio, I take a deep breath. The Wests' backyard is so dope. Like a mini-version of the Cummer Museum of Art & Gardens in town. Beautiful plants and flowers everywhere you look.

The first thing I notice is the singing—Maggie and her mom.

Tina West has a beautiful voice. It's a rich alto that flows beautifully beneath Maggie's high, controlled soprano. Any other girl with Maggie's voice would be looking for the nearest camera phone to record her talent and put it on the web.

Not Maggie. She'd rather get head lice than be caught singing onstage. However, she does some public performances. Like when she's braiding. It's the only time I see her lose herself in what she's doing so much that she isn't aware who's watching.

Which is why it's totally expected to see her standing behind Miss Tina's chair, doing her mom's hair. Maggie sweeps her mom's long, thick hair over her arm as she coaxes it into a single French braid. I smile at them.

"Hey," she says, waving.

"What's that?" I ask, getting closer. Before she can answer, here comes her sister.

"I did it. Now we match. See?" Then she shows me that they have a similar design on the backs of both their hands. "I'm Callie, by the way. You must be Daija."

"I must be," I say, looking from her to Maggie, whose eyes dart nervously around. She knows me well enough to understand I'd be suspicious of this new girl.

"Hey, Skipper is here!" Maggie's dad calls out, breaking the awkward pause. I like visiting the Wests. From the first day Maggie brought me home, I've felt like part of the family.

"Good morning, Tina, James," Kiki says, moving past me to plant a kiss on Tina's cheek.

"What's up, my people?" I sing out. I'm not going to be intimidated by this newcomer.

Her father cracks me up with his navy slang and dad jokes. Taz likes hiding, then popping out making kissy noises. And Mama West's easy laugh. She has a way of always including me, whether she's cooking or ordering takeout.

I'm as much a part of this family as anybody. At least, that's how I've always felt. Now, however, seeing the two of them side by side—Maggie and Callie—with their faces almost identical, it's a little shocking.

Not as shocking as seeing that Maggie is already accepting her before I can even figure out whether we can trust her! Callie might be okay.

But what if she isn't?

What if she tries to cause trouble? What if she tries to take Maggie's place in her own family? It could happen, right?

I realize Callie is talking to me, and I turn toward her. Homegirl is saying, "...if you like the henna on our hands, I can do one for you, too! They are super cool. My favorite artist, Anais, wears them all the time. So, do you?"

"Do I what?" I say, squinting at her like she's a math problem I can't quite figure out.

Maggie is finished with her mom's hair. She comes over and wraps one arm around my shoulders. She says, "Henna. She's asking if you want one, too." Maggie is chewing her lip and giving me the hopeful eyes—hoping that I like this girl, this stranger that we barely know anything about.

"Um, maybe. I'll think about it." Maggie gives my

shoulder a squeeze before letting go. I can see her big gray eyes begging me to be nice. I sigh, searching my brain for something "nice" to say. "Callie, your panda earrings are, uh, okay. They're nice."

I look at Maggie and hope she gives me credit for trying.

Maggie turns to Callie and says, "Hey, I noticed yesterday that you had a bunch of panda bear stuff—your backpack, your folder, even that case with your henna stuff has pandas on it. You must really love pandas."

"I've been into pandas since I was really young," she says. "What happened was, there was a girl in my school who said, 'You're mixed with black and white like a panda.' At first, I tried to laugh with everybody, but then they got meaner and meaner.

"When it kept happening, I started to get really sad. And you know how bullies are? The sadder you feel, the more they tease you. Well, this girl just wouldn't stop, so finally I told my mom. And she said I should stand up to this girl by owning it. I am Black and white.

"The next day, I went to school with a panda

folder and wearing socks with little pandas on them that my mom bought. The girl saw me the next day and once again started her teasing. 'Panda girl! Panda girl!' But instead of feeling sad, I told her I liked pandas and there was nothing wrong with pandas. I told her that pandas are worthy of respect like anybody else. Well, after that, it wasn't fun to her anymore, and pandas became like my own personal mascot."

Taz pops up out of nowhere and says, "Cool!"

Miss Tina says, "That was really brave of you, honey. I'm so sorry you had to go through that."

When I look at Maggie, she has that hopeful expression again. I raise my eyebrow at her, like *Can this girl be for real?*

Now they're all standing around, looking at Callie like she's the most precious thing ever. I can't stand it. I say, "Panda girl? For real?"

That pretty much ends the conversation.

Miss Tina says, "Kiki, you guys are going to have to leave in a minute. You and Daija should help yourselves to some orange juice or pastries and croissants over there. And sausage over here." She points toward the table.

"We had bacon," Miss Tina continues, "but a certain alien ate it all!

"Bloop-bloop-bloop-bloop!" Taz says, grinning.

Kiki, balancing a plate on her palm, turns and says, "Ooh, girls! I have a great idea. Why don't we invite Miss Callie here to join us at camp this summer?"

My brain screams *Noooooooo!*

I was really hoping to spend time alone with Maggie, discussing how to handle the Callie situation. I'm the one who has to look out for Maggie. For both of us!

"Kiki, maybe...," I begin, but Miss Tina is already nodding.

"That's a great idea, Kiki, thank you!" she says. Mr. West's head is bobbing and everybody seems super thrilled. Maggie is looking at me, all hopeful.

But I'm not ready to give in that easily.

"Kiki!" I say. "She probably has her own thing going on, you can't just roll up and start recruiting people. It's not the army."

"Hush, Daija. Callie would be a perfect fit. I bet the little girls would love to have their own henna tattoos. Are you interested, Callie?"

"I'd love to. Tina told me a little about the camp. I'd love to help if I can."

"Good!" says Mr. West. "And, listen, we're grilling tonight. Kiki, you and Daija should come over for dinner. We can all hang out back here." Kiki agrees. Then she walks over and places an arm around Callie's shoulders.

"I'd be happy to come, James, thank you. And Callie, welcome. I know the West family is happy to have you. And I'm sure you girls will all get along just fine!" When she says the "just fine" part, she looks directly at me.

I frown at her and start beckoning Maggie to come stand next to me. We have to show a united front. Everything is happening too fast. I feel weird and off-balance.

"*Psst!* Maggie!" I hiss. But scaredy-cat Maggie is acting like her feet are made of glue or something. See? That's why it's up to me to help her, even if she doesn't realize she needs help. That's what *sisters* do.

I let out a long sigh when I realize the matter is settled. Not like my opinion matters or anything.

To distract myself, I touch my toes, then stand up

straight and raise my left leg behind me until I can hold my foot. When I'm stressed, I stretch. I have to. It calms me down.

I continue pulling my toes toward the back of my head. A perfect scorpion pose.

"Daija!" says Taz. "That is *soooo* cool! I think the aliens on my planet should all do that, too."

Everybody laughs.

I inhale, smiling as I drop the scorpion, then stretch my ankles as I push onto my toes as far as I dare. Anytime is the right time to practice going en pointe.

Now, Maggie has seen me do this a thousand—a million—times. So, when I notice her eyeballs doing that darting thing again, I wonder what's up.

You won't believe it.

Callie is on the other side of me doing the same thing—stretching onto her toes, rising up and down from second position. Only, unlike me, Callie is practically on her toes. In sandals! The flexibility in her feet is amazing. When you've studied ballet as long as I have, you hear instructors talk nonstop about the importance of foot flexibility.

How is she doing that?

"I studied ballet for years. I was able to go en pointe really early. I can tell you're close. I could give you a few tips that helped me. Don't worry, you'll get there!"

Before, I'd been worried this girl might be trying to push Maggie aside and replace her. Now I can't help thinking:

What if she tries to replace me?!

CHAPTER 5

Maggie

The car is super quiet. No one is saying anything. Maybe that's a good thing? Maybe not.

Kiki is driving us to the camp. We're going to help set up. I know Daija like I know myself—soon as Kiki invited Callie to come along, I knew Daija wouldn't like it. Don't get me wrong, Daija is cool people.

But...

She can be a little bit, um, bossy and protective? Are those the right words? She likes for things to go her way. Most of the time, I go along because it doesn't matter as much. Something tells me, though, this summer the forecast may call for cloudy tempers and outbursts of rain—maybe tears, too.

Callie, luckily, has her face buried in her phone, so she doesn't seem to notice the big ol' wad of awkwardness seated between us.

Meanwhile, Daija is shooting weird looks at me in the rearview.

Thank God Miss Kiki finally interrupts the silence.

"We have two parks, right across from each other with a little lake in between. We're Heritage Park; the other is Paradise Park. At Heritage, we're arts and crafts; Paradise does outdoors activities like hiking, canoeing—that sort of thing. And Fridays most of the kids go on field trips with the Paradise folks. You girls follow, so far?"

When we mumble that we do, she tells us that we'll each be working with kids in our specialties. She says, "Maggie, I was hoping you and Daija could help the younger kids. You're so good with crafts, like friendship bracelets, crochet, and all of that. I can't wait for you to see the beautiful supplies they let us order."

"Yes, ma'am," I say. "We can do that."

She always tells me I can call her Kiki, like Daija does, but...I really can't. Even though Mom lets Callie call her Tina. I wasn't raised like that. It seems too weird.

"My mom made and sold jewelry for a living. I learned to do it to add to my allowance. I'd love to help!" Callie says.

In the mirror, I can see Daija roll her eyes. She told me already that we have to "check Callie out." What? Like we're private eyes now, doing a background check or something?

I glance away, unable to meet Daija's gaze any longer. I mean, it wasn't easy learning that I wasn't Daddy's only daughter. Then finding out she was arriving much earlier and probably for good. But you know what? I feel bad for her. She lost her mom. She's in a new place with new people. What I need now is to convince Daija that having her here could be a good thing.

We arrive and set about getting organized. Kiki leads us inside a building that looks like an old elementary school, but with better decorations. Like a drill sergeant, she passes out instructions and we head off with our marching orders.

"Let's get started!" Callie says, sounding super upbeat. I try not to cringe. I know without looking that Daija is going to roll her eyes.

"My, aren't you the cheery one!" Daija says, not sounding cheery at all.

Callie shrugs. "Life's too short. You've got to be happy!" Then she smiles wide, puts her earbuds back in place and carries her box to one of the long tables.

Daija uses her shoulder to push me in the opposite direction and starts harsh-whispering at me before I can even turn around.

"She's trying to push her way between us. I don't trust her!"

I groan, then pull her farther into the corner, away from Callie.

"*Shhh!* She might be able to hear you!" I fierce-whisper back.

"I don't care!" Her harsh whisper is getting harsher.

Shaking my head, I say softly, "Well, I do! We have no reason to be mean to her. You said you'd give her a chance. You know how you get when new people come around. It's okay."

"*Hmph!* You're so trusting, Maggie. I'm not saying she's a bad person. All I'm saying is we don't know her yet, so we need to keep our guard up."

We both take a breath, then plop our boxes onto a nearby table. Calmer but curious, I ask, "Why?"

"All I'm saying is you can't just go around trusting everybody. You have to make them earn it, that's all. And we don't know her, do we?"

"Well, no, not really, but..."

"But *nothing*. Just, let's get to know her before the two of you go skipping off into a field of flowers, holding hands and singing songs of sisterhood or whatever."

Now it's my turn for an eye roll. I sigh and say, "So long as you stop judging her and give her a chance to get to know us. Okay?"

"Okay!"

We both glance over at Callie but she's lost in her own world of beads and wires and, I'm sure, imagining all the things she can make. We decide to do the same.

The boxes I'm assigned overflow with colorful yarn and string, crochet needles of all sizes, and safety pins, which you need for marking your place and keeping up with the number of stitches. I find balls of thick, bright rubber bands, along with paper clips, rubber erasers, and colorful wires.

I organize my finds based on material, color, and function. Skeins of yarn in rich shades of red and orange and green and yellow are separated into one side. Bright and juicy colors so rich that I want to drink them.

What are we going to make with all of this? I'm suddenly overwhelmed with ideas. I grab my note-pad and pencil. "Callie," I say, going over and tapping her on the shoulder, "can I borrow your Surface? I want to look at Pinterest." Everybody gets ideas from Pinterest—even teachers.

She pulls the slim electronic tablet out of her beach bag, flips it on, and pulls up her pins and boards. One earbud dangles around her shoulder; the other sits in her ear.

"I love looking at pins for ideas, too," she says. "I'm listening to the radio. Did I tell you? Anais is doing this really cool thing this summer, surprising young business owners by giving them a shout-out or showing support to help them launch or increase their businesses! I love her!"

"We've talked about this, haven't we?" My voice is quiet but firm. She has dropped into an orange plastic chair next to mine. "No unbridled enthusiasm before noon. I can't take it. Okay?"

I give her the eyebrow. I mean, we did talk about it. Sort of.

She smiles at me and mimes zipping her lips, but I already know that zipper is doomed!

I type "crochet for kids" into the search box. I scroll. I scroll some more. Callie pops her zipper and begins chattering again. Then points. "Oooh! Click there!"

I click.

It's a page filled with colorful beads, yarns in mouthwatering colors, and projects for all skill levels. My brain *click, click, click*s away with possibilities.

"What are you thinking?" asks Callie.

"Well, I know most of the kids will be new to crochet, but I don't want to do just friendship bracelets.

I want to help them make something they'll really be proud of, you know?"

"Me too!" she says, getting high-pitched and giddy.

I give her a look and say, "Remember what I told you about being too giddy. It's still too early for that." I smile and so does she.

I flash her a stern expression.

"No, I mean it. No excessive giddiness."

But we both end up giggling.

Meanwhile, Daija is across the room noisily unpacking her box. I go over and ask how it's going. She says, "I can see you over there, looking all happy with your new friend."

"Stop!" I say, leaning into her shoulder. "We're getting to know each other. The same I way I want you two to get to know each other."

"I have a right to be suspicious."

Her box is filled with folders and papers and pens. We begin stacking them in neat piles. "But I don't think you need to be suspicious of EVERYBODY!"

She tilts her nose upward and says, "I think you're wrong." But finally, she smiles. A little one, but still a smile.

I don't want to spend my summer fighting. I don't want Daija mad. I don't want Callie hurt. I need for all of us to get along.

Daija, man, could you not be so salty. Please!

That evening, Kiki and Daija come over as planned. Daija has been giving Callie and I the cold shoulder most of the day. I had planned to talk to her about inviting Callie to be a Braid Girl, but I sort of never got around to it.

So, I am hoping we can clear the air in my back-yard. However, it doesn't exactly start out that way.

First of all, I get shocking-but-not-really-shocking news from my parents:

"Mama and the relatives are coming next week-end," Daddy says, way too optimistically. "Maggie, you know how long Mama's been talking about her trip to Africa. She has been collecting brochures for Nigeria since I was in high school. Well, she'll be there on the Fourth of July, during your birthday. So she wants us to have an early celebration for you so she can join in. That's good, right?"

I look at Callie, then back at my father.

"You can say it, Daddy. Grandma really wants to come here so they can all meet Callie," I say with a sigh.

"Not true," Daddy says. "Well, not totally true."

All I can do is shake my head. Callie and I exchange glances, and I shrug. It's not worth getting too bent out of shape over. Like I said, I wasn't exactly expecting it, but I'm also not exactly surprised.

Across the yard, Daija is pouting, stealing looks at Callie.

Then I get an idea. I tell Daija to join me at the trampoline. Callie is talking to Kiki. Daija does a vicious eye roll in their direction, then stomps off toward the trampoline. *Okay, so it's going to be like that, huh?*

"Why are you in such a huff?" I ask when we both climb up. We both sit crisscross facing each other.

"A huff? Me? I'm not in a huff," Daija says huffily.

"Come on, Daija. I know how you get about new people. Honestly, I still don't know how we ever became friends, knowing how guarded you can be. Were you ever this suspicious of me?"

When she looks at me, I'm expecting anger to flash in her eyes. Or sarcasm.

I'm not expecting the shimmer of tears I now see pooling in her eyes. "Oh, Daija," I say, reaching for her, "what's wrong?"

She swipes hurriedly at her cheek and pulls away from my touch. Her spine is perfectly straight, the way only a ballerina's can be.

She says, "I thought we had an agreement. I thought we agreed that we would take things slow with Callie and get to know her before deciding she's *our* friend. But then again, what do I know? I mean, you say we're sisters—you and me—but you guys actually *are*! What do you need me for?"

She crosses her arms and lets out a breath.

"Daija!" I say, grabbing both her hands. "You will always be my sister. You made me feel safe here. You helped me make other friends. You laugh at my jokes and don't make fun of my love of anime—the only good thing I got from living in Japan. I love you, goofy girl. We're fine."

She takes her hands away, but when she looks at me, I can tell the angry mask of emotions she'd woven onto her face is melting. A softer Daija waits underneath.

"Go on," she says, half playful, half suspicious.

I go on. "We talked about slowly getting to know her when I thought there'd be time. But plans changed. I was scared at first when the parentals told us that she was coming so soon. I practically didn't sleep at all. But after breakfast, we hung out in my room and talked a lot. Okay, she does sort of lean into the whole zen thing pretty hard...." Daija starts bobbing her head really low-key aggressively.

"But she's kind of nice. And just think, Daija. Her mom died like six or seven months ago. That's harsh."

Grudgingly, Daija starts to nod. "Yeah, that really stinks, I know."

"Sooo," I drag out the word. "Maybe you could just try to be nice while we're checking her out? Please?"

"Well," Daija begins, then pauses. "I'll TRY to be nicer, but if ol' sis over there gets out of pocket or starts acting sus, I might have to put her in her place. Deal?"

"Deal," I say, laughing, knowing that's Daija's idea of compromising.

She stands abruptly, causing me to tilt over on the rubbery floor of the trampoline. I quickly get to my feet and find my balance. I don't want her to bounce me out.

We both jump in silence for a while. I love jumping out here. The trampoline is where I go to clear my head. Daddy says it's more likely that all the jumping jerks my brain around. Whatever. It calms me. And after a little bit, it seems to have calmed Daija, too.

"I have an idea. A really, really great idea. For us. For the business," I say.

Daija backflips and lands perfectly, never stopping. *Jump-jump-jump!* She's waiting for me to go on.

"Your mom said we should expect girls between the ages five and ten. The majority of the girls at camp are Black or brown. Black and brown girls are our business. Why don't we offer braiding to the girls at camp?"

"For free?!" Daija screeches so loud that everyone goes silent.

A few moments pass before the family goes back to what they were doing.

"Not for free, Daija," I say, grinding out the whisper. "For money. We could set appointments after we teach our classes. Miss Kiki says that from two thirty to five most days we will have free time, unless our kids join the Paradise kids on some outdoor activity."

"But the camp is free. For underprivileged, inner-city kids. They don't have a lot of money," she says.

We've both completely stopped jumping.

"Listen," I say, "if we make a good impression during the camp, we'll have customers until Christmas and beyond."

"You really think so?"

"Girls in the neighborhood need their hair done, too. Working mamas will pay to get their kids' hair braided. All we have to do is come up with prices that work. It's worth a try, Daija. Don't you think?"

"Girl, I'm all about it!" she finally says.

She rushes off the trampoline and races over to Miss Kiki.

"Kiki, guess what? We have an idea." she says, and explains.

Her mom loves it and says it could definitely work. I take a deep breath, ready to tell Daija about me asking Callie to join us.

Only...

"Maggie! Daija!" It's Mom. "You have to include Callie! Look at her hair, with all the different shades of blue strands on the ends. It's artwork. And she says she did most of it."

I feel Daija's head whip toward me. Right on cue, little Callie-Wallie comes bopping over and says, "Tina, Maggie already invited me to join. I can't wait."

Daija, eyes bulging, pitches a fit, telling her mother that *she*—Daija—didn't come up with this business so she could split *her* profits three ways. *Hmm*...I thought the Braid Girls was *my* idea.

Daija turns to Callie and starts to say, "No offense, but me and Maggie don't—"

But that's as far as Daija gets before Miss Kiki talks over her, saying, "The idea is wonderful, and we're going to make Callie feel welcome. Aren't we, Daija?"

Kiki's jaw is as tight as the microbraids on her head.

"How wonderful, Callie," Daija says, sounding like one of those recorded messages, her face rigid. "Welcome to my...*our* business!"

All she'd need to make her robot face complete would be to add, "Bloop-bloop-bloop!"

❧ CHAPTER 6 ❧

Callie

We're all silent as we walk to the community pool in the subdivision. The grown-ups sent us on our merry way. We're supposed to work out the details of how we'll run the business.

My nerves are on edge, but I try to keep my cool. Deep breaths. I repeat a mantra in my head that helps keep my knees from shaking.

We're wearing swimsuits under our clothes.

I snap a selfie, then get an idea.

"Daija," I say, trying to keep the fear out of my voice. When she turns and looks at me, it's like death rays. Luckily, I'm wearing shades. I lift them cautiously. "Would you mind if I take some pictures of you and Maggie? I want my friends to see my half sister's best friend."

Maggie looks at me, then at Daija. She shrugs, then smiles brightly.

"Come on, Daija! It'll be fun," she says.

Now both of us are looking at Daija, who takes a long time before answering, "Okay, I guess."

At least, for now, the high beam lasers blazing from Daija's eye sockets have stopped. We walk along and some of the freeze thaws off her. They do silly poses in front of a few houses and with a few dogs on leashes when the owners say it's okay.

"I've always wanted a dog," Maggie says, grinning, then biting her lip like a shy kid.

Daija gives her wicked side-eye. "Maybe you should buy one with the million dollars you have stashed away," she says.

Maggie stops and puts her hands on her hips. I can tell they've had this, uh...discussion before.

"I do not have a million dollars. But I do have a savings account filled with money from three birthdays, six Christmases, and, of course, from braiding," Maggie says, looking satisfied. It's funny how she shifts from being soft-spoken and shy to giving her neck a swivel and looking someone in the eye.

Daija surprises us by turning to look at me. She says, "Maggie never *ever* spends her own money. Her parents pay for everything, and she doesn't have to pay for anything!" Daija tries to make her tone playful, but I can hear the thin thread of envy beneath hear words.

Is she jealous of Maggie?

We arrive at the pool. I shake my hair to free the small braids at my neckline. My swimsuit is bright aqua, which makes my skin tone pop.

My braids fall forward. I take the ponytail holder off my wrist and slide it over the braids, making a high pony.

Daija draws my attention when she removes her T-shirt without breaking stride. Her swimsuit is a hot pink two-piece. Heads turn as her long-legged self goes straight for the diving board, climbs up, and dives right into the pool, barely missing a kid floating past on his back.

Maggie is right behind her. Her swimsuit is a drab, one-piece tank suit—black. Maggie is a cool girl, but her clothes are so blah. I don't get it.

She tosses a glance over her shoulder, and the familiar wink of a dimple greets me before she follows in Daija's footsteps. However, her form when she goes airborne is better than Daija's. Maggie looks like she's in her comfort zone here.

Other people are noticing and paying attention, too. Daija may be the flashy one, but Maggie is multitalented and too shy to show it off.

Envy is so counterproductive. And bad for your aura. Still, I glance from Maggie to Daija before I follow suit on the diving board. I know my form isn't nearly as strong. A teeny bit of envy leaks in. Maggie really is sort of special. I want to feel that way, too.

We all splash around a bit. Every time I dive under the water, I expect I'll come back to the top and they'll be gone. It's a horrible feeling, and it makes me feel small. But time after time, they're still there. Finally, Daija climbs out and dries her braids with a candy-striped red-and-white towel. She raises the end of the towel to look at me.

"I guess it's time to talk business," she says.

Maggie produces the waterproof drawstring bag she brought along. Neon pink. The total opposite of her drab suit.

"Here," she says, passing a bottle of cold water to each of us. She removes a small notebook and pen, as well. "Let's sit down at one of the tables and just start talking about what we're doing."

We decide against the hard chairs around the tables and instead choose a grassy area where we can sit on our towels. Kids and families continue to enter and exit the pool area. The scent of chlorine carries a tang in the air. Squeals and laughter give the area a carnival feel.

"Okay, we all know *I* really need to earn money. Becoming a principal ballerina is not cheap. Plus, I have to earn a big role in the fall production. Auditions are coming up fast—late July. And if I get a part, we basically have two months to prep before the showcase," Daija says in a gust of wind.

"Why is this particular show such a big deal to you?" I ask. "I'm sure your studio puts on more than one show a year."

Daija sighs loud and deep. "Because, Callie"—she

says my name like it's synonymous with "clueless"—
"it...it just is, okay? I need this. They're combining
dancers from our studio with professionals. It's a
great way to be noticed!"

I get the feeling that if this were a movie, Daija
might be one of those dancers putting itching pow-
der or live snakes in another dancer's shoes.

Daija exhales, and when she speaks again, her
voice is calmer. "And, as you so kindly pointed out, a
sistah's pointe technique needs work," she says.

Oh. Didn't know it was a sore spot. My heart
is thumping. Why couldn't I have kept my big fat
mouth shut? Is that why she's been saltier than the
Dead Sea? *Hmph!*

Maggie says, "And I'm trying to earn enough
money so I can save and start other businesses. One
day, I want to buy property and charge people rent.
That's called 'passive income.' I can earn money and
watch anime from the comfort of my own home."

Both Daija and I look at her. Daija says, "Maggie,
girl, sometimes I think when you talk, a thirty-year-
old woman is somewhere deep inside your soul giving instructions."

We all laugh.

Daija comes across as the queen bee, but it's pretty clear that Maggie is the one with the ideas—and the one quietly in charge. Only, she does it in a way that Daija doesn't realize that Maggie has taken control, which is low-key genius on Maggie's part.

It makes me like her more.

Maggie says we should offer a limited menu of services, just enough to get us started. Daija disagrees.

"We don't want the girls and their parents thinking we can't do these complicated styles. I don't know about her," she says, nodding toward me, "but between you and me, we can do a lot of different styles."

"Sure," Maggie begins, her tone low and steady, "but if we want to do multiple clients so they can get the word around to as many people as possible, we could only do elaborate styles on a few clients in a day instead of simpler ones on many. Plus, the more elaborate, the more expensive, and like you said, most of these kids come from lower incomes. Think about it."

Maggie runs through the schedule that Kiki laid out for us earlier. She has a point.

"Realistically, we're looking at about a three-hour window to do kids' hair. From two thirty to about five thirty. I'm not sure we should promise we can do all this sophisticated stuff when, you know, it might make us have to rush. I think we'll get more customers and more done if we focus on nice, clean, neat styles that boys and girls like. I mean, don't you think so?"

"I agree," I say, because I do. Daija pulls a face, but I go on. "I think what Maggie says makes sense. Even if you guys let me work with you. And by the way, I work quickly, and I do good work, too. My friends back on the islands, they really like my box braids and my crochet braids. I can do a lot of styles...."

Daija looks from my face to Maggie's. She huffs, "Well, I guess it's two against one."

"No one's against anyone else, Daija. Come on. Listen."

Maggie runs it down:

- Choose styles suitable for kids ten and under for camp. (We can talk about doing hair for our friends and older girls later.)

- Jumbo braids or twists make a good choice, since they can be done quickly; a favorite is cornrows on the scalp that transition into twists on the bottom so the style will last longer.
- Cornrows, goddess crowns, box braids, pigtails, puff balls, and ponytails should be popular services.
- We will set our prices based on how intricate the design is. Basic cornrows or cornrows with add-ons start at twenty-five dollars. Box braids are forty dollars and up. Pigtails with cool parts are twenty dollars.
- We will work together to determine prices on other styles as we go.

Maggie takes a big breath. Daija does a world-class neck swivel and says, "Well, girl, is that it? Or do you have more rules and guidelines?" She crosses her arms.

"Not rules and guidelines, but numbers," says Maggie. "Take our lowest price—pigtails. We'd need to provide service to forty clients in order to earn eight hundred dollars. Which we'll then divide into three, which will give us two hundred sixty-six dollars and sixty-six cents each."

"Down to the last penny, Maggie, really?" says Daija, her tilted head signifying disappointment.

"Sounds great to me!" I say. Mom's life insurance, plus the money she inherited from her father and grandfather, now belongs to me. I haven't mentioned that to Daija. And I'm not going to. Even so, that's for later, like college. Or my first car. I still need money for regular stuff. I don't want the Wests to think I'm some kind of sponge. So not cool.

Daija cuts in, "What is this? *The Baby-Sitters Club*? You're coming at me with all these rules and everything. Don't I get a say?"

"Of course you do. This is simply what I've worked on. I'd be glad to listen to what you think," Maggie says, reasonably.

"Well, for one thing," Daija says, puffing herself up, "we need flyers. And lots of pictures for Instagram. I mean, a lot of pictures. Like this. See?"

She pulls out her phone and opens Instagram. Within seconds, images of styles pop up. I open mine, too. I spot pics of friends, hairstyles I've done or helped with, Mama Conch at the Conch Shack—everything from friends to the jewelry that Mom and I made. Just seeing a few of the pieces gives me a lump in my throat.

Maggie says, "Did your mom make those?" She's craning her neck to see over my shoulder.

I nod, not trusting myself to speak. She gently takes the phone from my hand, and she and Daija flick through my images.

"The designs are really pretty," Maggie says, handing back my phone.

"Thank you," I say.

I scroll, my palms sweaty, showing more photos. Then I come to several images of braid styles I'd done for friends.

"See, this girl." I point to a plus size dark-skinned girl with gorgeous, thick braids. "I did her hair. And the other girl, Sasha, my best friend, I did hers, too. If you have any photos of styles you've done, we could post them."

Maggie bounces her eyebrows at Daija, a slow smile pulling at her full mouth.

"We do have a few photos. We'll need to call their moms and make sure it's okay to use their pictures online and even on our flyers," Maggie says, hesitantly.

I add, "Daija, if you'd like, I can do the posters and the notices or whatever. But that's only if you want me to. Or I could help you with it."

She eyes me like I might try to take over the business. Am I sweating under her laser gaze?

"Well...," she begins, but my nerves take over and I jump in:

"I can upload the pictures, and we can make some flyers as soon as we get back to the house," I offer. "I'm great at making posters on the computer. I used to do it for my mom's business all the time. Mama Conch, too."

Daija, who's been holding on to her stank face, finally exhales and gives me a smile. "I love me some conch chowder," she says.

I beam.

"Me too!" I say. "Maybe I could make it for us sometime."

She gives me a nod that says *Maybe*. I'll take it.

Back at the house, we announce our intentions. The grown-ups look like they are relieved we've returned alive. Maggie goes over to James, and he reflexively leans over and kisses her forehead.

For just a second, Daija and I lock gazes.

One look at her now, and I know for a fact, at this moment, we're thinking the same thing:

Maggie is so lucky.

But I'm going to make my own luck.

I'm going to give this business everything I've got!

CHAPTER 7

Daija

I am feeling totally Gucci.

As in sick, as in dope, as in—bang-bang-*bangin'*.

That is because Callie has real skills when it comes to designing posters on the computer and making them look professional. We sent them to the print shop yesterday after she finished. Now me and Kiki are stopping to pick them up before we pick up the girls.

Soon as I see our new flyers, I'm like, "Dang!" She did a good job. It's my first big step toward showing my father that I'm not the same little kid goofing around in a tutu. I'm serious about my business, my studies, and right now, ballet.

Heritage Park and Paradise Park share a big traffic circle—well, not a circle, more like a U-shape. It's one way in and one way out with a large plot of grass in between, but sidewalks that go around the U. It's a pretty park that I've visited many times over the years.

We start the morning passing out our new flyers as parents drop off their campers. Maggie keeps track of things with her little clipboards and paper, and Callie is using her powers of chitchat for good rather than boring us with Anais facts. We begin booking appointments before camp even gets started! That's so dope!

Then a car pulls up and I'm like, "Oh, yeah!" One look at Maggie, and I know she is seeing what I see. A white lady with her brown hair pulled into a bun pulls to a stop in a sweet ride, with four little Black girls inside. Biracial? Adopted? No matter.

She looks frazzled. When she helps her girls out of the car, they look so sweet, but *honeeeeeey*, their heads are jacked up. Taking care of Black girl hair is no joke. And if you don't know what you're doing, well...

"They are the perfect clients!" Maggie whispers. She does that thing, tucking her lips in, trying to hold back her smile—and hide her braces. But the dimples are as deep as wading pools.

"Girl, they need us," I whisper back.

I start my speech. "Good morning, I'm Daija. This is my friend Maggie and the girl over there, that's Callie. We're junior counselors, and..."

My voice falters for a second. I don't want to come off like, *Lady, you need help!* Black girl magic starts with our hair. And this mama needs a magician.

Maggie surprises me when she pipes up. "We do hair." She passes a flyer to the lady.

Finally, I find my voice and say, "We call ourselves the Braid Girls, and we're offering special discounts for campers who get their hair done here. Are you interested?"

That woman looks like she wants to fall on her knees and shout "Hallelujah!"

Next thing you know, we have customers for the entire afternoon.

We sign up more clients, mainly for later in the week. Most of the parents want to wait until

Thursday so the little mamas will look good at church or birthday parties over the weekend.

When the cars pulls away, I can't help myself. I do a perfect twirl. Then a leap, too. I can feel myself being swept up in the excitement.

Callie dances over and breaks the spell. She says, "That was great work, you guys!" I still say she could be sus, but I can't help grinning, and soon the three of us look like we're posing for selfies.

I do another twirl. Callie does a twirl.

Then Maggie asks, "Callie, you said you stopped taking ballet classes once your mom got ill, right?"

Callie's whole face seems to sag in that moment. But after a second or two, she inhales, draws herself up, smiles, and answers, "Yes, that's right. I'm hoping to get back to it, though. I loved taking dance."

She looks at me when she says the last part. Okay, I'm not heartless. I'm not saying she's totally in, but... her situation is tough. I smile at her, thinking maybe I'll invite her to my class.

Maybe.

Everything is off to a super, fantastic start, and I'm not doing anything to blow it.

But you know what? Some people just can't stand to see you shine.

Soon as we turn around, here come three chicks in Paradise Park camp tees, stomping toward us.

"Whatcha'll doing over here?" says Lorilee. The other two, Ciara and Angela, stand slightly behind her, forming a triangle—of doom.

This is a *verified* shade party.

"Um, we're over here, at Heritage Park, where we belong, minding our business. Uh, what about you?"

From the corner of my eye, I can see Maggie take two steps back. Angela and her salty ways might scare Maggie, but not me.

"And who are you again?" Callie pushes her way forward, looking at all three. Unlike Maggie, Callie doesn't seem to have a problem standing up for herself. I have to admit, I like that about her.

"I'm Lorilee, and I'm a junior counselor at Paradise Park Summer Camps. Ciara and Angela are junior counselors, too," she says.

"Well, nice to meet you. I'm Callie, and we're junior counselors at Heritage Park. How nice for all of us!" she says with her beaming white smile. Is she serious? Or is she, like, goofing on them? It's so hard to tell with Callie.

Ciara, who has to look up at me, begins pointing her finger and swiveling her neck. She says, "We're just making sure that you Heritage Park girls stay in your lane—'cause we're watching you." She actually does that thing. You know? Where you point at your eyes with two fingers then aim them at the other person? Oh. My. God.

"How lovely!" Callie is saying. And in her sweetest voice, she adds, "We'll be watching you, too!" Then she flashes the biggest, widest smile. The shade party scrunches their faces like they can smell their own feet.

Then Angela decides to step up, ignoring Callie and turning to me, saying, "You're *counseling* this summer, too?"

"Angela! How good it *isn't* to see you," I say. Callie covers her laugh with her hand.

"Ha-ha. You're *sooooo* mature, Daija Renee." They all stand there, Paradise Park T-shirts tied up on one side. So last year.

Most of the cars are pulling away from both sides

of the circular drive separating the park entrances. It is called the Big Lawn, and Kiki says this year if there are events involving both parks, they'll most likely take place there.

Angela pulls her arms tightly around herself, and says, "I know you're not stealing customers from us!" The Big Lawn area separating the two parks looks like a big green ocean. It makes me wonder how these girls got over here so quickly.

Once again, Callie cuts into my thoughts with a valid question:

"What customers? Are you selling something?" she asks, using her sweet voice again.

A late arrival rolls up. The driver lady grins when Callie hands her a flyer. She says, "Thank goodness! You girls are just what I need." All the kids who climb out are wearing Paradise Park tees.

Maggie appears from the background and stands beside Callie. She says to the woman, "Thank you, ma'am. Check the contact info on the flyer if you need help outside of camp hours. I'm sure we can make it work."

"Honey, I will be emailing you before the end of

the day. Save some time for us on Thursday or Friday 'cause my baby don't want to go to the field trip," the mom says.

Lorilee snatches a flyer from Maggie, who instantly looks like she wants to shrink away.

All the parentals agreed yesterday that email is best for contact with the public, although they are allowing us to use our phones with customers once we've met with them.

"*The Braid Girls*?" Angela squawks, throwing more shade than a spa umbrella.

"Good name, right?" I say. "And now we know that Angela can read!"

The look on Angela's face is *everything*! Even Maggie coughs up a chuckle or two.

Angela is throwing death rays with her eyes, but it's her girl who speaks first.

"Y'all can't be stealing parents from our camp to braid their kids' hair!" Lorilee says.

Maggie frowns. "Do you have a braid business, too?" Her eyes are big and round and I can see she's totally serious.

Angela snarls, "We can if we want to!"

"Y'all don't even do hair. One look at your heads tells us everything we need to know," I say.

Maggie, the peacekeeper, frowns. Keeping her voice low, she says, "D, that's not cool. You shouldn't make fun of their hair."

"Shut up, Nerd Girl," Angela snaps. Maggie tucks her lips and looks down.

Kiki and another adult are talking nearby. They start walking our way. Kiki and the woman reach us. Maggie looks *sooo* embarrassed, and those Paradise Park chicks look like they don't have a care in the world. *Hmph!*

"Hello, I'm your camp director, Coach Lori," says the tall woman with Kiki. She wears a whistle and a name tag.

"Ciara? Angela? Lorilee? Now, what are you doing on this side of the traffic circle? Shouldn't you girls be at your tables greeting our summer students?" the tall woman asks, her voice pleasant but with a hint of "don't make me repeat myself" to it. She turns, pointing toward Paradise Park. "I think you'd best get some pep in that step. Come on, ladies!"

The three girls grumble, "Yes, ma'am," before marching off like a miserable band of deserters.

So that was the jump-off.

Fast-forward.

Me, Callie, and Maggie all help each other with our individual classes. Maggie teaches a basic crochet stitch so the kids can make friendship bracelets before they learn something more complex; I lead a group of kids in dance stretches. Callie knows a little *sumthin'-sumthin'* about computers, so she is making that happen.

I have more fun here than I'd thought I would. Meeting new people, laughing along with the girls... it is a fun first day.

A few hours before the end of the day, it is time for our appointments. Me and Callie each have one client, while Maggie agrees to do two.

Summer afternoons in Tangerine Bay are often rainy, but today the weather is sunny and mild. An ocean breeze keeps the air silky.

"Let's sit outside, back here," I say, leading them

to a path on the back side of the camp. Kiki knows about it and says it is cool if we go back there.

We stop beneath a canopy of golden rain tree branches with their delicate yellow blooms. A carpet of petals covers the ground. Beyond is a narrow band of blue water separating Heritage Park and the rear of Paradise Park.

"Oooh! It's so pretty back here," says one of our little clients.

Maggie shares a warm smile. "D, it's beautiful," she says.

"I know, right? I made it myself!"

Everyone laughs, except Callie, who goes quiet. I look over, seeing her face at an angle. She looks like she is remembering a happy time.

Then she exhales, and it looks like all the light in the world just went out. It only lasts a few seconds, but it is sad to watch. Then she catches me staring, quickly swipes a tear from her cheek, and gives me her best smile.

She takes a deep inhale, closes her eyes, exhales, and says in her sunshiny way, "No energy can disturb the peacefulness of my body."

I look at her, then look away.

CHAPTER 8

Maggie

The next day, when we arrive at camp, we are greeted by those horrid Paradise Park girls. They are standing at the end of the U-shaped curve, glaring over here with their arms crossed and stank faces firmly in place.

I inch up beside Daija, take a quick breath, and say, "Whatever they do today, please, please, please just ignore them. We can't have potential clients seeing us arguing with other counselors. Not a good look, you know?"

"I know!" Daija snaps. Then her tone softens and

she says, "Sorry. They just work my nerves. But I'll ignore them today." And despite their glaring and whispering and pointing like they're laughing at us, Daija keeps her word.

We manage to get through morning check-in without any other run-ins with Angela and her crew. We're doing classes outside today, under the pavilion, which is covered. It's nice out, and the kids are down with it, so it's cool. I brought out the supplies earlier with Callie's help. However, when I reach our pavilion, I can tell instantly that something is different. What is it?

"Daija, Callie, come here," I say.

"What's wrong?" asks Callie.

"Look around," I say. "Something is different." They both frown, of course. But together we go through my boxes filled with yarn, paper clips, large-eye needles. But something feels off. It takes a minute, but soon I figure it out.

When you crochet larger pieces, you need safety pins. I haven't used them with the kids yet....I turn to the other two girls and point.

"Look!" I say. "Right over there." They look at a jar of slime sitting on the table that the kids play with.

One of the favorite camp activities is to make slime. Kids love it, and it's not too hard to make. The slime in the jar is old and breaking down. It's more liquid than gooey.

And most important of all, it's not ours. I didn't put it there. And I definitely didn't put a hundred-count pack of safety pins inside!

"We know who did this, right?" Daija says. Already, she's on fire. Hands on her hips, lips pressed flat.

"Well, we can assume, but I don't think we should jump to conclusions," Callie says in her sunny, sing-song voice. "Besides, we need to stay positive. Feel-good energy." A smile is plastered on her face, yet her body language says she's mad. I am getting along with her just fine, and I like her most of the time. Sometimes, though, I really, really, really need her to actually *be* calm instead of just talking about calming down.

Daija throws Callie a look. I decide the best thing

I can do is redirect the energy. Mom is a school-teacher. I've learned all about redirecting kids when they are being "challenging."

"Braid Girls," I say, "we don't have time for this. We need to have a little chitchat about business."

That gets their attention. They drop onto picnic table benches across from me. We have a few minutes because the coach is leading the campers through morning calisthenics—that's what she calls it, anyway.

"What's up, girl?" Daija asks, looking stressed. I hold up my hands.

"Nothing tragic or dramatic, D, so, you know, keep it chill. I just want to talk about our duties with the clients this afternoon. Not to mention the people who've already emailed."

Daija and Callie nod. I lower my voice and we put our heads together.

"We have five clients today, but two are boys wanting cornrows. Now, for tomorrow, Thursday, we've got six clients. However, Thursday evening we've got three kids coming to my house. Daija, we'll need you," I say. "Any ballet on Thursday night?"

"I'm good, baby girl. I'm there!" And just like that, no one is thinking about the girls from Paradise Park anymore.

It's not long before little ones clamor into the pavilion. I begin my crochet class. I ignore the gross-looking sight of the safety pins floating in the gelatinous goo. Of course, it's the first thing one of the kids notices.

"Hey, that's cool, Miss Maggie," says a little girl, about five years old.

"You think?" I say.

She nods confidently. And when I look at the jar, I decide the gag backfired. I've got plenty more safety pins.

I shift my focus. The campers have their little crochet needles.

"Remember, carefully loop your yarn across your pointy finger, hold your needles like this," I say, demonstrating, "and pinch the loop we made earlier. Yes, now insert the needle into the loop. Good. And catch the yarn that's hanging free with the hook of the needle, and pull through, just like this."

I watch their little faces as they create their first

loops. They look like they've discovered new worlds built of candy. A really strong feeling fills my chest, and I'm surprised to realize it's pride.

Seeing these kids learn, being part of it and teaching them something, makes me feel proud of myself. Daija is off helping a group of tiny dancers, so Callie is helping me this morning.

We each walk around, checking the campers' work before I lead them to the next step. Later, when she does her jewelry making class, I'll be her helper, too.

"Kids," I say, "we've been practicing how to make chains and then circles, right?" I see a lot of nodding heads.

They're all just so cute and sweet. Well, most of them. "Lucy, leave Madison alone. You focus on your own work, okay?"

"Okay!"

She's not a bad kid, Lucy. But I've noticed that she struggles with the crochet needle, then she gets frustrated. That leads to her wandering around, causing problems with other people.

"Lucy, come here," I say. I take out a larger needle

and some fatter yarn. "Let's try this needle. Maybe it'll work better for you." She looks curiously at the fat Q hook, but she takes it.

"Look, everybody! My needle is the biggest!" she says.

Wonk-wonk. So much for trying to appeal to her softer nature.

I tell her, "Lucy, please avoid teasing the other kids. Everyone chooses needles based on what they think they can use. I think this one might help you. Now take your yarn and go practice, please."

"You're very good with them, Maggie," Callie says. "I'm learning a lot from you. I...I really like that."

Callie drapes her arm around my shoulders. Then she stands up straight, sucks in a bunch of air, and starts breathing it in and out. She says, "This is how we cleanse our souls! You can't hold on to the negativity of others. That's what Mom used to say. The Paradise Park girls are washing us with bad energy."

"*What?*" I say.

One of the girls sitting nearby lays down her yarn and comes over to us. She grins, patting my shoulder, and says, "She means those girls over there"—she points her little finger toward Paradise Park—"are troublemakers. My name is Rhyse."

She wraps her arms around my neck and squeezes. "I'm glad I'm at your camp and not over there with them," she says. "Those girls, they're not nice. You make us all feel special. Thank you, Miss Maggie."

I hug Rhyse back, and she returns to her seat, picks up her yarn, and goes on like nothing happened.

Callie whispers, "Told you! You're amazing with them, Maggie."

Out of nowhere, I lean into Callie and bump her with my shoulder. Believe me—for me, that's big.

"Aw, shucks," I say, trying to play it off. "I'll bet you say that to all your sisters."

She snorts out a laugh.

"You snorted!" I say. Several kids heard her, too, and they're laughing and smiling.

"Miss Maggie," says one of the older girls sitting toward the front, "are you and her sisters? Y'all do look alike."

Callie and I look at each other and smile.

"We are, and we do," I say. And oddly, saying it

makes me feel closer to her. I mean, it's only been a few days, but I am trying.

And so is she.

Daija?

Wellllllllll...she'll come around. I think.

We lead a small group of kids to our braiding spot—Mystic Cove. Kinda cheesy, but it's what Daija calls it, so I'm good with it. In the distance, thunder rumbles, but it sounds like it's moving away from us. If the storm turns this way, an alarm will go off, letting us know to get the campers inside.

My clipboard is firmly in my hot little hand. I feel like a proper businesswoman! Although maybe a little sweatier because of the humidity.

Daija, Callie, and I decided that we won't try to boss one another. We all have a specialty—mine is organizing the schedules and supplies, Callie's is media and advertising, and Daija is an excellent braider and even better talker. She'll make sure we hustle up customers.

The campers are marching along, some singing,

some dancing, some off in la-la land. They don't seem to mind the gray skies.

Dariella, my client and a real sweetheart, squeezes my hand. "I don't like thunder," she says.

"That's okay. I'm not a fan of it, either." I say. She tries to smile back, but I can feel her tremble through her small fingers.

Callie must've overheard because she joins us on the path. She leans down to Dariella and says, "Oh, you don't need to fear thunder. Listen, all you have to do is count the number of seconds between thunder bursts. If it takes longer and longer between crackles of thunder, it means the stormy air is moving away. See? Listen."

Dariella looks up at me. I nod at her, and together we listen to the rumble shivering through the clouds and into the earth. Sure enough, when it thunders again, I can already tell that it sounds farther away. Dariella can tell, too.

After that, we settle into our regular spot and two more clients, Zach and Trey, in serious need of cornrows, rush toward us, waving their arms and their matching plastic dinosaurs.

The boys race around us, and all I can think of is Taz and his goofy robot ways. So, I stick my arms straight out and go "Bloopee, bloop-bloop-bloop!" I know, it's totally ridiculous, but at seven, ridiculous is their language.

The boys open their eyes wide. Trey says, "Cool!" When I look around, everyone is cracking up, me included.

"Dariella," I say, "I'm going to do your hair first. Then, Zach, it's your turn. Then you, Trey, okay?"

They all nod.

A little time passes, not long, and I finish with Dariella's hair. No cornrows, but instead little girl ponytails in rows of three in back.

"What do you think?" I ask, passing her a small hand mirror. Dariella smiles.

"Pretty!" she says. That makes me happy.

"Okay, I need to do Zach's hair," I say.

"Can I stay over here with you?" she asks.

"Absolutely! I was hoping you would keep me company."

Zach seems like an old pro when it comes to getting his hair braided. He plops down on the beach towel as soon as Dariella moves into the lawn chair beside me. I get started.

His hair is twice as thick as Dariella's. We should've charged his mom more, but too late now.

I get lost in the task of perfectly parting his hair and keeping the wide cornrows neat, so I don't notice that three more guys have joined our group. That is, until a deep voice fills the air.

"You do good work! Would you do mine sometime?" says the voice.

I look up, and a boy with copper skin and wide, greenish-gray eyes is looking at me. I open my mouth to speak, but the awkward immediately takes over.

"Um, uh, huh?" *Smooth, Maggie. Real smooth.*

He squints at me, but his smile is still warm.

"I'm Keith Montez. I'm a junior counselor, and Zach is one of mine," he says easily. Keith Montez, I realize, is wearing an identical shirt to Zach's. Paradise Park Camp. It's a radioactive shade of green. My heart is skipping around. *He's so fine, he's so fine, he's so fine, doo-dah, doo-dah!*

He pulls up a folding chair right beside me. I do my best to keep my cool.

"So, um, you're...uh, why are you here?" My voice cracks.

He pushes out of the chair and says, "This is a nice little spot you've found over here. And look, right there"—he points through the murky grayness of the afternoon toward Paradise Park—"that's our supply area. I think the girls over there, some of the junior counselors, are cooking up something. They're a trip."

I peer into the milky cloudiness that has floated in, covering up the sunlight, and squint at the brick building. Then Daija pops up out of nowhere and scares the holy sweet macaroni out of me.

"That's part of your camp, right?" she asks Keith. Before he can answer, she nods and says, "At Paradise, right? I wondered what that building was!"

"Daaaaija," I say, on high alert, "what are you thinking?"

"Just gathering intel," Daija says, adding an evil laugh.

Intel? What?

When I look back at Keith, he's staring at me. I swallow hard. Aw man, his eyes are so pretty.

"Um...," I say. Staring into his eyes, I feel my brain totally disconnect from my mouth. "You braid want me do?" Yup! That just came out of my mouth. Is there a reset button on life? I need a do-over.

"Sorry," I say.

I practically shove poor Zach off the beach towel and wave Trey over. His hair is really long, but his mom only wants me to put a little oil on his scalp, detangle him, and give him a cornrow crown.

Instantly, I hide my hot face behind Trey's bushy hair, wishing I could hide somewhere, anywhere.

Trey, remembering my time as an alien, looks up at me and says, "Boop-boop-boop," and grins.

When I peek over at Keith again, he looks as shy as I feel, staring down at his shoes, cheeks turning a warm cinnamon that's apparent despite the gray daylight.

Is awkwardness contagious? I mean, did I awkward all over him so hard that he got infected? Is there a cure? A vaccine?

"You...you really do a good job. I'm...I mean, I was serious. I'd really like it, for you, I mean, to do my hair," Keith says, not quite making eye contact.

"Oh...I um, er...uh okay," I manage to say, each word sticking like peanut butter to the roof of my mouth.

Callie and Daija are watching, giving me looks. I turn away, but not before Daija flashes me her "get it, girl" grin. I will not engage in her foolishness. Nope!

I'm finishing Trey's hair when I see them. I gulp, mouth to Callie, "Here they come: the girls of Paradise Park. Waiting to pick us apart."

CHAPTER 9

Callie

Soon as I lay eyes on those girls, I know it's not going to be pretty.

Maggie looks close to hyperventilating. I've been trying to teach her to breathe for relaxation, but not the way she's doing it. I try to give her a look of encouragement, but I don't think she notices. We all fix our eyes on the Bermuda Triangle headed our way.

Angela doesn't waste any time. "Trey!" she practically barks that poor boy's name. "Did you let *her* braid your hair?"

Wide-eyed, Trey looks from Angela to Maggie

and back again. He stammers, "I—I—My mama said for her to do it."

"Who are you, again?" I ask, my sweetest voice in place, fighting the itch of anger clawing beneath my skin. I force myself to laugh. Not for any reason other than I feel more like screaming.

I need Mom. I need her here to help me find calm. More and more, I'm starting to feel out of control, but I made her a promise after she died: I vowed to find peace. I have to try harder.

She completely ignores me and gives all us Braid Girls the hand. "*Psshhh!* Whatever," she says. "Trey, and all the rest of y'all Paradise kids, tell yo' mamas you don't have to come over here no more because we have our own hair braiding business. Why would you need the Braid Girls when you can have the Sistahs Who Braid?"

"What?" Daija explodes.

Angela sneers. "Yeah, I said it. We're starting our own braiding business at our own camp," the girl says. "You can stay on your side."

I tilt my head, and even more sweetly, I ask, "Who did *your* hair?"

"Like I said before, who asked you...*white girl*?" Lorilee snaps.

I hear Maggie gasp. Even Ciara and Angela turn their faces away.

"Lorilee!" says Ciara, scolding.

I feel my face flame red. The whole panda episode at school comes to mind. I've gone through this before, but it still doesn't mean it doesn't hurt now.

"Don't be rude and ignorant, guys, come on. You're better than this," comes the shocking response from Maggie Marie West! "She's biracial. And just so you know...she's my sister!"

Maggie moves beside me.

Her sister.

A wave of emotions washes over me.

Keith, who I've almost forgotten, moves carefully to stand by Maggie, too.

Angela, hand on hip, says, "I know you're not trying to crack on nobody!" Then they cackle like three witches.

Out of the corner of my eye, I can see Keith look at Maggie, concern etched on his face.

Angela laughs the loudest. You can tell where

bullying is concerned, she's not a newcomer. Her eyes are still on Maggie.

"I can't believe you even have the nerve to try to start a business," Angela goes on. "Everybody knows you can't do nothing for yourself. That's why Daija is always fighting your battles. You ain't got no back-bone, and you don't know how to stand up for your-self! Just a crybaby."

"She's more like the Cowardly Lion," Lorilee jumps in. More laughs go around.

"Angie, Angie, Angie," says Daija. "You need to get over yourself."

I can't help myself. I say, "Now that I'm seeing your hair up close, too, Angela, uh, hmm...your parts are crooked!"

Anybody who braids knows that crooked parts are a no-no!

"Yeah, well, let's see how good we keep our parts when we steal your braiding business!" Lorilee sneers. "You can check out our Insta, @sistahswhobraid, and you'll see what we can do!"

Buses and cars arrive, and the squeal of air brakes drowns out the Sistahs and their jeering laughs.

A breeze kicks off the ocean a few blocks away and blows a salty, humid breath in our faces.

Angie grabs Trey by the hand and practically drags him away. She says to him, "Tell your mama to come to us next time if she wants somebody to do your hair."

Maggie, her eyes wide, presses her full lips into a flat line. She's not making eye contact with anyone, not even Keith, who doesn't know what to do with himself.

"Guess I'd better get over there and help the kids get ready to go home," he says, not looking at anyone in particular. Maggie looks close to tears. Keith shoves his hands deeper into his pockets. "Hey, I'm sorry—about those girls."

"It's not your fault," Maggie says softly.

Then he smiles, and the two of them get all moony-eyed. It's adorable.

Daija, looking fit to be tied, jams her hands on her hips and says, "Um, excuse me. You two are precious, but those girls are gonna pay. I'm going to make sure of that!"

It's not what Mama would've done, but, well, I can't say I disagree with Daija.

In fact, I think sooner or later, we're going to have to put them in their grubby little place!

Camp finally ends for the day. I'm feeling like I've been on a roller coaster—going up and down, down and up. Each day, I miss Mom more and more. Even though Maggie is being nicer, everything feels so hard.

James is taking us out to dinner. Daija comes, too. With Taz, Maggie, Daija, and me squished in the back seat, I'm feeling claustrophobic.

I put my earbuds in before the SUV even pulls out of the parking lot. I can't think straight; I need to clear my head, and my mantras are not doing the job. When I hit Play on my radio app, Anais is belting out my favorite song of hers—"Searching for Atlantis." I've sung the lyrics so much that they feel like home.

When we arrive, I'm the first to jump out.

I'm glad to be outside.

"Callie, you must be hungry," Daija says, "because you never move that fast!" I look over but don't say anything. They've been teasing me, saying I'm on island time. But I'm not in a joking mood.

I'm homesick tonight. Missing my friends, my old neighborhood—everything.

It's a seafood restaurant, which I think is nice, since I told James and Tina I love seafood. And it's on the water. We're led to a table outside on the deck. Boats skim across the harbor.

One deep inhale of the briny air, the seafood cooking in the distance, the faint smell of oil from some of the boats—and I'm back in Nassau, back home.

The memory hits me so strongly that the first thing I feel is the urge to spin around and say, *Mom! Look!*

But when I turn, she isn't there.

Maggie is there, however. And she has maneuvered around me on the restaurant's back deck so that once we're seated, I'm sitting next to James, with Taz on his other side, and she's sitting between Tina and Daija. Maggie is smiling to herself, studying the menu and making small talk.

She engineered this!

I wonder if James is as uncomfortable as I am.

"Are you okay?" he asks softly. When I look up, he's staring down at me, concern in his warm gray eyes. He reaches down and takes my hand. "Good thing we wound up next to each other; gives us a chance to talk a little."

Taz sings out, "Bloopity, bloopity, bloop-bloop-bloop!" And when I look at Maggie again, she is out-right grinning.

"What are you having, Callie?" Maggie asks.

"This place is so dope!" Daija cuts in.

"I love this restaurant," Tina says.

"Bloopity, bloopity, bloop-bloop-bloop!"

For a few minutes, I stare out at the harbor. Boats with triangular sails move quietly across the flat surface of the water. An orange-and-gold sun is dipping lower.

I need to center myself. That's what Mom always did when she felt, in her words, "adrift." So, I breathe in, breathe out. In and out. And I repeat something Mom taught me to do when I'm sad—especially after she found out she was sick. I repeat, silently:

I will feel better.
I will feel better.
I will feel better.

The tang of the salty air, the happy jitter of conversation, the bloops of a joyful robot—and the soothing scene and my mantra—all of it fills me. Then I feel a breeze, a soft brush of air that moves across my skin. I feel it move through my whole body.

And for just a little moment, I smell the dusky scent of Mom—her perfume, her incense, her cooking.

"Maggie," I say, feeling better than I have all day, "I am having the conch fritters, and some grilled snapper. I love snapper. And maybe some clam chowder? I looooove clam chowder!"

Maggie bursts out laughing. "Look who's feeling better, I guess." Her voice has its usual wry tone, but she's not shy smiling anymore.

"I don't want anything grilled," says Daija. "I want fried shrimp, french fries...and can somebody fry my salad?"

Everyone laughs again.

The conversation continues well after the food arrives. Tina and James are talking about taking us somewhere, like down to Disney or Universal. Tina asks if I've spoken with Aunt Lana—I have, but only briefly.

James nudges me with his arm, the same way I've seen him and Maggie nudge each other a bunch of times in the short while I've been here. When I look up, he's looking down at me, smiling.

Then he reaches onto my plate with his fork and steals a fritter. "Hey! No fair!" I say, even though I only sort of like them. They don't compare to authentic Bahamian conch. But I've been having too good of a time to complain.

With an expression that looks a lot like Taz, he gives me an "uh-oh" face, pops it into his mouth, and says, "Sorry," in a not-sorry-at-all tone.

"Daddy," Maggie groans. "Don't be weird."

Tina pats her daughter's hand.

"He can't help it, dear. It's just who he is!" And we're laughing some more. I still can't get over that feeling that swept through me earlier. The feeling that my mom was here, with us. And then sitting with James beside me and Maggie not upset or anything.

By the time we leave, I feel something I haven't felt in a long time—I feel wanted.

CHAPTER 10

Daija

It feels so good paying my tutor with money I earned. All my stretching and practicing is paying off. With each day, I am getting closer to my goal— earning mo' money, mo' money, mo' money, to pay for more classes and show my father I'm for real.

Miss Honey, a principal dancer with a national ballet company, doesn't waste any time. "Let's go to work, mama," she says.

My muscles are still warm from a free studio class I took earlier. That was mostly stretching, with runs and leaps for endurance. Working with Miss Honey—that's all about strength and muscle training.

It feels great, working out all the kinks and stresses of the week. Feeling the Sistahs Who Braid and their dirty tricks move through my muscles, out my fingertips and toes.

While we change into our pointe shoes, Miss Honey says, "I know these extra classes can be expensive. I love your drive, your commitment. If you know anyone who wants to split the session with you, it would help you with the cost."

I immediately think of Callie, even though I'm not sure if I'm ready to have her in my space like that. So, I simply nod and tell her I'll think about it.

I get my foot positioned in my shoe, wiggle it to make sure I can feel the support.

"Are my ribbons tied right, Miss Honey?"

She isn't much taller than me, but she's strong. In her black spaghetti-strap leotard and pale tights, every muscle in her shoulders, arms, back, and legs flexes and moves as effortlessly as water in a fountain. Miss Honey bends just enough to lift my foot and examine how I've tied my ribbon.

She approves.

At the barre, we go to work. "Remember," she says, "being successful en pointe is ninety percent mental."

For the next hour, Miss Honey takes me through a ballet vocabulary list of movements—first position, second position, tendu, plié, relevé—a series of moves designed to build my strength so I can balance my weight atop the boxes in the toes of my pointe shoes.

"*Sous-sous!*" she calls out, directing me to swiftly bring both feet out and push onto my toes. I follow her commands, again and again. The muscles in my leg are taut. Dancing makes me feel joyful. Something about it—the music, the way ballet teaches you to control your body, the feeling of being light as a feather—all of that makes me want to dance forever.

By the time we finish, I am soaking wet with sweat and my calf muscles are on fire.

"Get some water, mama. Hydrate," Miss Honey says. "Good work. You've got everything you need—except the confidence. You'll get there."

I sit on the floor, back to the mirror wall, and take out my insulated water bottle. My throat feels so dry, like I've inhaled all the dust and resin in the room. I take a big gulp and go for a second one when I notice my phone blinking.

The ringer is off—you never EVER let your phone ring during a ballet lesson. Never!

I see the notifications.

It's my father!

"Hey!" I almost shout into the phone after punching Redial.

"Did I get you at a bad time?" That's my father, all business. No "Hey, girl," or "Hello, beautiful," just right down to it.

"No, Dad. I'm just finishing my ballet class. I've got time." In the room around me, light piano music plays softly. Miss Honey is talking to another dancer from her company.

My father's voice has its usual crisp baritone. "Good. How are you doing in school?"

"Dad, it's summer break. No school." Goodness! He forgets everything about me.

"Sure, sure, that's right," he says. "I am sorry I had to cancel our dinner this week, but I want to see if you have some free time a week from Saturday?"

Whenever I am on the phone with my dad, I feel rushed. Like I have so much I want to tell him, but when he calls, I get...not tongue-tied, more like brain-tied. All the thoughts and feelings come rushing at me so hard that nothing comes out.

It feels horrible to want so badly for him to spend time with me like he used to when I was his only child.

"Really, Dad?" I manage to say. I want to say yes, yes, yes. And I'm about to when I realize that's the day of Maggie's birthday celebration. I feel all the air rush out of me. "Sorry, Dad, but I've got Maggie's party that day."

"That's fine, we can do it another day. You should be with your friends." Part of me wonders if he's relieved. The thought makes me feel miserable. "By the way, what are you doing tomorrow?"

I frown because he's already canceled dinner for tonight. Hesitantly, I answer, "Nothing, really, other than stretching, working on my pointe. I don't have any classes, though."

"Excellent! I figured if you weren't doing anything tomorrow. We could bring your brothers over, and you could braid their hair. You and your little friend.

The girl whose father is in the navy. I spoke to Kiki. She said she's fine with it as long as you want to do it."

Air rushes out of my lungs. I am like a balloon the day after a birthday party. Not quite forgotten, just not as important.

My cheeks feel hot. He doesn't want to see me. He is only in need of braid services for his precious sons. I feel bitter and angry, and I know that is not a good look. Besides, I like hanging out with the little guys. They aren't so bad. I tried hating them, but I just wasn't any good at it.

I let out a deep sigh. I wish I could say:

Dad, I had an amazing class. My ballet teacher says I'm really showing improvement. I'm doing all of this so that I can earn a starring role in the fall showcase. I want you to be proud of me, Dad, like you used to be when you'd carry me on your shoulders into the ballet classroom and sit there with the other moms and dads before you and Kiki split up. I miss you, Dad.

"Daija? Daija! Are you still there?" His voice crackles through the phone. I look up and see Miss Honey tapping the face of her watch, an apologetic look in her eyes as she signals she has to leave.

And I see Kiki in the doorway. I can't make eye contact with her. She knows already what he's saying to me and one look of "I told you so" might send me over the edge.

"Yeah, I mean, yes, Dad, I'm still here. I heard you. I've got to go. Kiki's here."

"Well, we'll see you tomorrow, then."

I push off the floor, grab my things, and say goodbye to Miss Honey. Kiki never says a word. Her silence is worse than any words she could have spoken.

Later, at bedtime, when she sticks her head in my door and says, "I'm sorry, baby girl. I'm sorry," it hurts worse than when she goes in on him with all the reasons why they had to break up and everything.

I nod to her as I shut off my light. "I know, Kiki. I know."

"Your brothers have gotten so big!" Maggie says on Saturday afternoon. She and Callie come over to our townhouse. And they've brought Taz along, too.

"I know, right?" I say. We've taken over the living room and dining room. Believe it or not, Kiki likes having the boys over. It isn't the first time I've done their hair or earned babysitting money from watching them. But it *has* been a while since the twins were here.

At least I've pulled myself together. I have to get my mind right. Ballerinas have to be steel butterflies—graceful, light on their feet, but strong and tough.

My brothers and Taz are playing a video game. We are helping Kiki clean up after the chili she served.

Maggie dries her hands and drapes an arm around my shoulders. "You're a good big sister, Daija Ryan," she says. She leans in, resting the side of her forehead against mine.

"Aw, shucks!" I reply.

Callie smiles. "You two are silly, but Maggie is right, Daija. That was really nice of you, helping him out like that. Your dad, I mean."

I feel a whole lot better than I felt last night. Me, Callie, and Maggie go into our tiny backyard, and Kiki sends the boys outside, too.

"Let's play Safari," Taz says. "My granny is going to Africa."

"I know how to walk like an elephant," Justin says.

"Lions are my favorite. *Grrrr-owww!*" says Jayden.

The three of them run around being wild beasts. Maggie says, "They remind me of that book I used to love so much, *Where the Wild Things Are*."

"Oh my goodness!" exclaims Callie. "I loved that book, too!"

We go on like that, chitchatting about books and stuff. We have a portable speaker set up to a streaming radio service and when Callie hears Anais singing, she gets all starry-eyed.

"You're a trip, you know that?" I say to Callie, but I smile.

"How did your session go with the tutor?" she asks.

"I can tell I'm improving. Miss Honey says so, too. It's just...I don't know. I get nervous, which makes me wobble. And nobody got time for a wobbly ballerina!"

"My old teacher used to say pointe work was ninety percent mental," says Callie.

"Miss Honey said the same thing!"

Kiki sticks her head out the patio door. "Boys, come get your stuff. Your dad is here." We all tromp back inside, helping the boys gather their things.

Out of the blue, Callie turns to my dad and says, "Mr. Ryan, Daija is an amazing dancer. You must be very proud of her."

It's so embarrassing I want to shake her!

My breath catches in my chest and I go still. My father, wearing one of his casual suits—Kiki used to make fun of him for wearing suits all the time— looks from Callie to me, then back to Callie.

"Of course. I know my daughter is very talented. And a hard worker. I know she'll make an excellent ballet dancer or whatever she puts her mind to."

His tone is businesslike, but he smiles at us and I feel myself exhale. Maybe he does notice me.

As quickly as he answers, he turns his back, focusing once again on the boys outside.

When they are gone, I realize I've been biting my lip. I do that a lot around him.

A lead role in a professional-looking ballet performance open to the entire city. That would make him notice me. He'd notice and not look away. He'd have to. He'd really, *really* be proud.

I tell Kiki we are walking to the Wests' house. Maggie asks me to sleep over, and Kiki says it is okay.

Callie is on her phone, pushing buttons and frowning. She does that a lot. Always checking her socials, doing her *thang*! I look at her—really look at her. Sometimes it just feels like her zen stuff feels made up, or like she's trying too hard.

But sometimes she is just pushy enough. Like earlier in the week with those Paradise Park girls. Then Wednesday at dinner. I saw how truly happy she was sitting next to her father.

I am surprised Maggie is so cool about it. But she has been telling me that she's really trying. She feels terrible about Callie's mom. Maggie has a big heart like that.

Maybe it's time I ease up a bit and give Callie the benefit of the doubt. If she does something shady, I could always go back to treating her as sus.

But I have no idea how I'd be acting if something happened to Kiki.

Maybe all her mantras aren't just some act.

Maybe they are how she is coping with everything. And maybe she isn't out to push me out of the picture and take my place as Maggie's best friend.

Maybe.

With a deep breath, I say, "So, Callie, if you're still interested in taking some pointe classes, Miss Honey says we can share the class—and the cost. What do you say?"

CHAPTER 11

Maggie

Monday, when we are getting ready to leave for camp, Daddy pulls me aside in the kitchen while Callie finishes up her hour-long shower. And she claims to be trying to lower her carbon footprint.

"COB," he says, "how's it going?"

He's peeking around the corner, like he's on lookout at a top secret base. Sometimes, Daddy can be so extra.

"Daaaaaaaddy," I say, dragging out the word.

"Your sister..."

"Half sister," I correct. He grimaces.

"Callie. How is it going?"

I tell him it's going fine, but he gives me a look.

"Baby girl, I'm asking how are things between you and her? How are the two of you getting along?"

"*Ooooooh*," I say, "I like her, Daddy, I really do. And I'm being extra nice, just like you asked me to."

"Magnolia Marie..."

"I am, Daddy, I swear."

Then a serious question occurs to me.

"How are you and Mom doing? About this whole thing, I mean."

"Your mom is amazing. She never wanted Callie to come here on a trial basis and stay with Lana, anyway. All along, she wanted her here right after Clover died," he says with a soft smile.

"But you didn't?" I ask. We're both standing with our backs to the countertops, holding matching glasses of OJ.

"No, it's not that. I...I was worried about you. Both you and Taz, but you mostly. I knew this was a lot, and I didn't want you to feel overwhelmed," he says. He looks at me with a bit of concern. "I still don't."

I throw myself against him in a hug that sloshes juice from both glasses. He laughs and pushes me away playfully, saying, "Now I'm sticky!"

He grabs a paper towel, wets it, and rubs over where the juice spilled. When he speaks again, I can hear the hurt buried in his soft words.

"I am Callie's dad. Why her mother kept that from me all these years, I don't know. But I want to be here for her, you know?"

"You *are* here for her, for all of us. You were great at the restaurant the other night. I think she really enjoyed sitting next to you. Give it some time. She'll be all right. We all will," I say.

I hope I'm right.

That was the good part of the morning. Too bad it went downhill from there.

We arrive at camp and are greeted by those horrid Paradise Park girls and their even more horrid signs:

SISTAHS WHO BRAID

PARENTS, SIGN UP YOUR KIDS
FOR TRENDY STYLES FOR LE$$ MONEY

Kiki, who disappears after we first arrive, comes back and sees us gaping at the posters being held up across the big traffic circle separating the two camps. She looks at Daija, then pastes on a big smile.

"Girls, guess what? Coach Lori was so impressed with your braiding idea that she is making a big announcement this morning," Kiki says.

Coach Lori calls most of the counselors and junior counselors to a grassy area.

"Good morning, young people," she says, her counselor shirt tucked neatly into her khaki shorts. "I have news for you." We gather around her. She continues, "I'm happy to announce that thanks to the initiative shown by a group of young ladies at Heritage Camp, we are bringing in a guest speaker on Thursday to discuss how kids can start a business."

Daija, Callie, and I look at one another. Then Coach Lori says that our "ingenuity" was so impressive that we've inspired girls at Paradise Camp to launch their own business, too.

Daija whispers, "You mean inspired them to steal our business."

I shush her and keep listening. Meanwhile, heat is rising off Daija in waves. Especially when we see the Sistahs Who Braid over there taking bows. Shameless. What else can you say?

"Well, it might be nice to get some advice from a professional, don't you think?" I ask the girls. Callie agrees. Daija rolls her eyes.

It would have been okay if the news had stopped there—but it doesn't.

"And, young people, we're doing something special this year for our campers. We're having a mother-son, father-daughter dance at the end of the summer. Not a formal dance. We want you and your parents to have fun. You can even make up a little dance beforehand. But you can also just dance. No pressure..."

My first reaction is to smile because I can just imagine Daddy trying to get his dance on, and I

pray to goodness Callie wants to dance with him—
because I certainly don't.

However, Daija goes gray.

She looks like she's been shocked by the battery-
operated paddle Daddy zaps mosquitos with in the
backyard.

"It'll be okay," I whisper her way. But one glance
at her face and I know she doesn't agree.

So, that is how Monday morning ends. On a weird
note. And on Tuesday, the tune doesn't get any better.

It turns out, the Sistahs have stamina.

Because that morning, we discover that the Sistahs are already stealing our customers. Several of
our appointments are canceled by the end of the day.

By Wednesday, feeling like captains of a sinking
ship, we ask Mom if we can go hang out at the beach
after camp. Let off some stress. Revive our summer
of fun!

Mom drops us off near the boardwalk. "Be back
by seven thirty and I'll meet you here," she says.
"Don't forget to use your sunscreen. Especially you,
Miss Callie!"

She's using that special "mom tone," so you know

she's not playing with us. No unauthorized sunburn on her watch.

I love it at the beach and can't wait to spread out my beach towel, put on my sunscreen, and stare at the ocean. We'll all relax. Play and have some fun. At least, I hope so.

"It's so beautiful out here," Callie says.

I look at her and say, "Remind you of home?"

She nods. "Definitely!" I glance at Daija, hoping a change of scenery will lighten her mood. Based on the smoke plumes curling outside her ears, I'm going to say no.

"You guys, we've got to do something about those Sistahs," Daija huffs as we drop onto our towels and begin hoisting the huge sun umbrella we brought from our garage.

"What can we do?" I ask. What I want is an afternoon away from business and idea thieves and worry. Just good old-fashioned fun.

"I think we should focus on the positive," says Callie.

Daija mimics, "'*Focus on the positive*.' You're like a walking Hallmark card. Don't you ever give it a rest?"

Even Callie looks taken aback. Both she and I stare at Daija. I say, "C'mon, D, no need to point your anger our way. Let's talk about it if it's bothering you so much." Not that I want to talk about it. I want to forget about it.

But it doesn't look like that's happening.

"Well, it is bothering me '*so much*,'" she says, now mimicking me, too.

She lets out an exasperated grunt before crumpling onto her towel. Shadows from the umbrella play across her face.

"Maggie, you and Callie don't need this like I do. I really, really need it. I love paying for my ballet tutoring on my own. I'd like to continue. But how is that going to happen if we have those bullies running around trying to blow up our thing?"

Callie is wearing a white two-piece with one blue stripe along the side. She let me get my hands in that hair, which I'd been dying to do. Now she's got two Bantu knots in front, then a part at the back where it's cornrowed down to her nape, then the braids hang. So cute.

She rubs sunscreen into her arms and legs, saying, "Those girls definitely need a vibe check, that's for sure. But, Daija, you have to believe that they don't have the skills to back up their words."

"So what? We're supposed to sit around not earning money, losing customers, until people get wise and realize, 'Oh, yeah, they really do suck'? That could take forever!"

Here's what I've learned—when someone is itching for an argument, you might as well let 'em get it out of their system. Daija doesn't want to feel better. She wants to fight.

I know what this is really about. The father-daughter dance. I mean, Daddy will dance with her, no problem. I even told her that yesterday.

Still, Daija's only response to dancing with my father at the dance was to turn a cold shoulder. It's turning into Mount Everest around her.

Buying time, I finish applying my own sunscreen, slide my sunglasses down my nose, and lie back against the pillow I brought. Callie talked me into this bright blue two-piece. I can't tell you the last time I wore a two-piece. But I'm not feeling too bad in it. With my shades on and my hair styled, I'm feeling kind of good about myself.

"Daija, please try to relax. It'll all work out. You'll see," I say before taking Amanda Gorman's *The Hill We Climb* out of my bag and flopping back onto my pillow.

I lie back with the book against my body, edges worn from being handled so much, and close my eyes and imagine a world where I can be my own version of Amanda Gorman—a young Black poet who stood before millions during a Presidential inauguration.

The sun is a white-hot eye peering from behind burning clouds. The tangy aroma of the ocean fills my insides, and silky breezes curl from the shore, which flicks warm waves toward our toes.

I know we have things to think about, strategies to figure out. Still, I also want to have some fun.

"Callie!" I say, dropping my book. "I'll race you to the water. Last one in has to be nice to the Sistahs tomorrow all day!"

She tears away from her towel, and I do my best to trip her, push her, or otherwise get in her way. Our laughter sounds like singing sea birds.

"Daija! Come in! The water feels so good!" I call to her, waving my arms. Callie keeps repeating that she won and I have to be nice to the Sistahs, even though she knows I made it into the water first.

My best friend uses her hand as a visor, makes eye contact, then snatches her thin frame away from us. That's cold.

"Guess she's not in the mood for a little fun," Callie says.

I think about the thieving, conniving Sistahs. I think about real sisters who show up and raise each other up.

And I think about friends with stubborn streaks, goals, enemies, and moving past adversity—about Amanda Gorman's gorgeous speech on a blustery January day.

I'm not sure if I'm ready to change the world, I think. But little by little, I can feel I'm changing myself. Each day, a little more of the scared girl I have always been falls away. I wrap my arms around myself and twirl knee-deep in the ocean.

I won't let Daija's bad mood take over me.

I won't be bullied by the Sistahs.

I will speak up for myself. I'm sure I can. I mean, I will.

A sigh escapes me.

At least with Callie, the uncertainty I'd been feeling about her is melting away. Daija can be suspicious all she wants—that's just how she is. We'll get through this whole Sistahs thing together, like family. Like friends.

CHAPTER 12

Callie

By Thursday, it doesn't take long to see that the Sistahs Who Braid have declared war. It feels like there aren't enough "namastes" in the world some days.

They're over there, strutting around with big poster board signs. If I weren't working on my kindness and moral center, I might point out that their posters look like they were made by kindergartners.

Still, watching them prance around trying to be us is enough to make my hands itch and my eyes twitch.

Like Daija, I am feeling hot and bothered and

would love nothing more than to plot some tasty payback.

I shut my eyes and repeat a mantra Mom used when she was feeling agitated.

I am in my body....I am connected to this earth....I am anchored like the roots of a tree.

The phrases string together in my mind and roll off my tongue in a whisper. Despite not fully believing in the process while she was alive, I feel myself grow a little more quiet inside.

Coach Lori's voice cuts through my thoughts.

"I expect my campers from Paradise Park and Heritage Park to be on their very best behavior," she says in a sunny, camp cheerleader kind of tone. "Our guest speaker will be here shortly, and I want you all to behave accordingly."

We break into our normal morning groups. Instead of helping Maggie, I'm leading a group of kids in yoga.

I wonder if Mom knows how hard I'm trying to keep my promise to her. And I wonder, what would she think about that?

I sigh and try not to giggle as the kids attempt

yoga poses—from tree to triangle to mouse—on wobbly little legs.

Daija and Maggie bring their girls to join my morning yoga group. Maggie, casting a quick glance at Daija, says, "I thought we could all use a little spiritual enlightenment this morning."

Daija gives a nasty snort. A few kids giggle; a few others look a little weirded out by all the attitude Daija's throwing.

I drop my butt onto the ground to get into a lotus position, press my palms together, and guide everyone through a new series of stretches. "Remember, today is a new day," I say, repeating something Mom loved saying to me. I hope the children enjoy it like I did when I was their age instead of resenting it the way I did later.

"Breathing is important," I continue in my happiest yogi voice. "It helps you release the negativity trapped inside you."

I try not to laugh as I peek and see several little kids struggling to get into good lotus form. I push to my feet, walk around, and gently guide their limbs. Most sit crisscross applesauce. But a couple of the little dancers working with Daija actually get their feet in the proper position.

We go through a few more stretches, and by the end, everyone seems more relaxed. Well, the campers, at least. Maggie, too. Daija...she still looks like she wants to bite somebody.

Mia, one of Daija's little dance students, who is sitting in a perfect lotus position, asks, "Miss ladies, are y'all gonna let those other girls start doing everybody's hair? 'Cause I don't want them doing my hair."

Daija rushes over before I can even open my mouth.

She says, "Don't worry, little mama, no one is going to let those...uh, *girls* get near you!" She has her hand on one hip, feet firmly planted, and finger out.

Maggie says, "Don't worry, Mia. You're our camper, and as long as you and your mother are good with it, we are your braiders."

The morning flies by, and everyone is excited to hear the speaker. Okay, maybe not everyone, but I am. Maggie, too.

"I'm not happy how it came about," Maggie whispers as we plop down on our beach towels along with our young campers, "but I am excited to hear what a real business professional has to say."

Most of us sit on beach towels in the grass. Daija sits on her knees, arms crossed tightly.

With an exaggerated eye roll, Daija says, "I just want to get this over with. We need to plan. I can't let my business get upstaged by...*them*."

"You mean 'our' business, right?" Maggie says, softly but with an edge.

"Yeah, whatever!" Daija waves her off. *Hmm*...it's not the first time she's slipped and called the Braid Girls "her" business. Maggie looks like she wants to believe it's a simple mistake, but deep down, she has to be thinking the same thing as me:

Daija has convinced herself that she *is* the Braid Girls!

I look over at Maggie and give a tentative smile. She smiles back, her face mirroring mine.

Saturday, her—our—relatives are coming over for an early birthday celebration. I've been sneaking around, working on something special for Maggie's birthday. I can't wait to give it to her. I really, really hope she likes it.

But...I am worried about meeting everyone. Just when I'm starting to get the feel for the family here, they bring more people into the picture. The only grandmother I've ever known is Mama's mom, and that was hardly a storybook relationship, because my grandmother is the one person Mama couldn't tolerate.

Feedback from the microphone makes all of us flinch. Coach Lori apologizes, then introduces the speaker, a tall, elegant woman with her hair swooped into a French roll.

Her pantsuit is robin's-egg blue and she's wearing the cutest little bracelet ever. I can't help wondering how it's made and where the jeweler got her supplies.

The woman's name is Evelyn Marks. She says she has owned businesses since she was six years old. "I love talking with young people about owning their own businesses and learning how to be responsible, independent, and motivated," she says.

Maggie has her notepad and pen ready for action, and as Ms. Marks speaks, I can see Maggie writing furiously to keep up.

Ms. Marks spends an hour breaking it down.

- Start small; be flexible.
- Choose a business you're passionate about.
- Make a business plan.
- Be organized and prepared.
- Communication skills are important.
- Understand that failure is part of the process—learn from your mistakes and move on!
- You have to make mistakes. DO NOT BE AFRAID TO LEARN!

Maggie has circled "Communication skills are important." She also circles the last one, about making mistakes and moving on.

She says, "She is awesome! I wish Ms. Marks taught a whole class for kids on starting a business. I'd take it!"

I can feel the happy energy rolling off Maggie and it makes me smile inside. She's gonna love my gift to her, I just know it!

Daija is another matter. Now she has both hands

on her hips and is ferociously whispering, like she's in some kind of spy movie.

"Listen," she says, and Maggie and I pull back to steer clear of the spit zone. *Ew!* "Sure, that chick said some cool things, but what we need is a plan to get rid of the Sistahs Who Braid. You feel me?" she says.

"Daija, she's a grown woman. A grown, professional woman. Don't call her a 'chick.' You know better than that," Maggie says, her tone uncharacteristically scolding.

Maggie and I exchange uncomfortable looks. After listening to Ms. Marks, getting back at the Sistahs feels less important than looking for ways to make our own business better.

Coach Lori comes back to the front and tells everyone to give a warm round of applause to our speaker, which we all totally do. She really is amazing.

Ms. Marks moves to the microphone again and says, "I'm going to come back next week to coach you all—counselors and campers. I want you to spend the next several days thinking about what it is that you love to do. What are you good at? How can you use it to start a business? It was a great idea to start a braiding business. Who came up with the idea?"

"We did!" says a voice. Not Daija. Not Maggie. And not me. It's that Angela, looking smug. "Some other people tried to start theirs, but ours is way better!"

Lorilee agrees, saying, *"Mmm-hmm!* Ours is much better!"

Daija turns and practically leaps toward Angela and her friends, but Maggie grabs ahold of the back of her camp shirt and pulls her down.

"What?" Daija screeches. "You think we should let them get away with telling their lies? That's not right!"

"I think," Maggie says, "that it's not worth it to our business or reputation to cause a big scene in front of the guest speaker."

"They have got to be put in their place!" Daija says.

I don't want to make a scene any more than Maggie does, but I am getting tired of the Sistahs, too. Daija is right about one thing—something has to be done about them. Soon!

CHAPTER 13

Daija

We're at Maggie's later that day. Thank goodness we still have clients coming, thanks to our posters.

Before the clients arrive, we sit in Maggie's room while she goes over some information.

"I just want to say," she begins, "that I really loved learning from the speaker today. She made some excellent points that I think we should consider."

Callie is bobbing her head, but I stay silent and motionless with my arms crossed. Maggie continues:

"I love when she talked about learning from

failure. I think there are things we can learn right now from this Sistahs situation," she says, causing me to practically choke.

"You're not serious, right? You're not trying to turn this nightmare into a teachable moment?" I huff. Back at school last year, we had this social studies teacher, Mr. Herriman, who was always trying to take ridiculous things kids in our class did and "turn them into teachable moments."

"Yes, Daija, I'm serious."

"Maggie has a point, Daija," says Callie, working my last nerve again.

Okay, I can't take it anymore.

"What point, Callie? What point do you think she has?" I look back and forth between them, feeling myself spinning out of control.

"Daija, calm down, okay?" says Callie.

"Don't try to use your yoga voice on me. I. Am. Not. The one!" As in, not the one to mess with, not the one for anybody's reindeer games.

"Daija!" says Maggie.

I feel myself losing it. I can't help myself. I go into a full rant.

"You know, Maggie, we might not be having this problem if you'd just learn to stand up to people and weren't so afraid of fighting back."

Maggie slides off the side of her bed and comes to stand in front of me, sitting in my beanbag.

"And what does my behavior have to do with them starting their own business?" Now her arms are folded, and I don't think she looks afraid at all.

But I can't stop myself. I pop up, mirroring her posture. Most of the time, Maggie is so mild-mannered. Always trying to diffuse a fight. Not this time. Right now, she is mad. But I'm madder.

I raise my finger and say, "Look! All I'm saying is, if you weren't always trying to be so nice and everything, maybe that first day when the Sistahs were talking smack we could have shut them up for good. Then maybe we wouldn't be having this problem now."

"Oh," says Maggie, taking a step back, "so this is all on me? Because I wanted you to show some self-control and not let the senior counselors and all the arriving parents see you acting just like them? Is that my biggest crime? *Huh?*"

"Well, you said it, not me!" I snap. It doesn't totally work for what we're talking about, but it's all I can come up with.

"Daija, what you're really bent out of shape about is the father-daughter dance. Instead of biting everybody's head off, why not just ask your father?"

That stops me cold.

Right at that moment, her bedroom door opens. Of course, her dad is standing there, smiling, with a kitchen towel over his shoulder and smelling like the spaghetti sauce he's been busy making.

"Girls," he says, "two of your little clients are here."

I feel myself close to tears. I'm shaking, I'm so upset. I sputter, looking from him to Maggie. "Did you ask him yet? Did you ask your father? What about Callie? Who is she going to ask? Of course your father is going to say yes. He never says no to his 'COB.' Unlike..." My voice breaks, and I know this time I'm gonna lose it for real. Breath catches in my throat as I finish my thought. "Unlike my father. Right? Is that what you're thinking? Well, I don't need your pity. I can't believe I turned down my father's dinner invitation for Saturday because of your party! I'm out!"

"Daija! Wait!" Maggie calls.

I brush past her and her father, who looks super confused. Before I can get ahold of myself, which I've clearly been struggling with for days, I'm running out the door, grabbing my bike, and riding away.

Kiki isn't home when I get there. I know she'll be surprised when she does, because she is expecting me to be at the Wests' until later. I go straight to my bedroom, throw myself on my bed, and sob uncontrollably.

What am I going to do?

CHAPTER 14

Maggie

Thanks to Daija's little blowup yesterday, and because our clients had been waiting for us, I have to explain to Daddy now why she'd been yelling at me. Thank goodness we don't have to go to camp on Fridays. I need the break.

Both Callie and I explain the basics, telling him about the Sistahs Who Steal Clients and how uptight Daija has gotten about the whole thing.

Then I have to break down and tell him about the dance. *Oh man!* You should see his eyes. Big saucers of glee.

"You mean we get to *turn up* on the dance floor?"

He really does say "turn up." He's doing an old-man dance, probably from the nineties. Make it stop. *Sigh.*

I have to come up with something, quickly, because (a) I do not dance in public, and (b) I was not going to "turn up" at camp with my goofy dad doing his impersonation of someone with dance moves.

"No, Daddy. I think you and Callie should do something together." *Sorry, sis!* She has that deer-in-the-headlights look. Having a sister is good.

Daddy throws his arms around both of us and squeezes. "Don't worry, girls. I promise I'll be a perfect date for both of my daughters!" Then he runs like a little kid, shouting, "Tina, Tina, guess who got invited to a dance!"

It's now Saturday, and I haven't spoken to Daija at all since she went running from the house. I couldn't believe she left us there with five clients total. And I really couldn't believe she never called, texted, nothing.

It's the longest I've gone without talking to her since we became friends. But every time I even think about calling her to make up, I feel a hot streak of anger I didn't know I had start to bubble.

Callie says, "Don't worry, Maggie. I'm sure she'll be all right once she calms down. I'm positive." She sounds "positive," but I'm not so sure.

Today is also my faux birthday, and we're being invaded by relatives eager to meet the newest member of the family.

A birthday party on my non-birthday with my over-the-top family will actually be a welcome distraction.

"Happy birthday, sweetheart," Daddy says, kissing my cheek. Put Daddy behind a grill and he's in his happy place.

"It's not my real birthday, Daddy." I hoist a tray of marinated chicken thighs and wings and follow him to the outdoor kitchen. His pride and joy.

"According to Mama, today *is* your birthday. So, you know, what Mama says…"

"Daddy, stop. You're not a kid," I say, lowering the heavy tray to the concrete countertop.

He uses his long-handled fork to pierce the meat and plop it onto the sizzling grill.

"COB, you'll learn that no matter how old you get, when it comes to your parents, you'll always be a kid!"

The yard fills up with loud, hungry relatives. I can feel the tension rising off Mom. Her fear for her beautiful garden is real. So far, everyone stays on the stone walkways, content to admire the deep purple and hot pink bougainvillea bushes climbing the back fence.

And even though I know they aren't here entirely for me, once everyone arrives—especially my cousins Amber and Alana—it is...*pretty okay*. Maybe better than okay.

Except for Daija.

And come to think of it, Callie's been acting a little weird today, too.

I go up to her and ask, "Hey, are you getting nervous about meeting everybody?"

"Um, sort of," she says.

"Don't be. It's Daddy's relatives, and most of them are just as corny as he is. You'll be fine," I say.

She smiles, but somehow, I think something is still wrong. Callie has been so excited about a present she has for me, something she's been working on since last week. Today, however, she hasn't mentioned it at all.

I've watched how Mom and Daddy look at us when they don't think we see them. I'm not naive. I can tell how important it is to them that we all get along—but especially me and her. I thought we were. But something's up today.

With Daija being MIA, I need Callie to be her regular old self. I feel shaky enough having Daija mad. Maybe standing up to her wasn't the right thing to do. Maybe I went too far.

Most of the relatives have been here all afternoon. Now the sun is draining out of the sky, when someone comes up behind me, covering my eyes with their hands.

"Who is this?" I say. I blink away dots from having my eyelids pressed down. Then I twist my head, opening my eyes to see it's my cousin Amber. "Hey, girl!" I give her a hug.

"Cuz, now you're gonna know what it's like having an older sister," she says, glancing at her sister, Alana, who waves.

"Callie is only a few months older than me." The whole "big sister" thing feels too weird. I'd rather think of us as mismatched twins. Simpler.

Amber laughs, whispering, "That chick over there is only a year and a month older than me"—she glances again to Alana—"but that's never stopped her from bossing me around." Amber has a habit of calling people "chicks."

Gram gives Amber's arm a pinch.

"Ow! Gram!" Amber squeals.

"Watch your mouth, young lady. Always calling people 'chicks.' Manage yourself!"

Grandma is hard-core. Amber tries to pout, but Gram doesn't care. She sticks her tongue out at Amber, making the little kids—everyone really— laugh. Amber is only playing like her feelings are hurt, anyhow. She grins and as soon as Gram walks away, she looks at Alana, turns up her nose, and mouths, "Chicky, chicky, chick-a-dee!"

It's a good party, even though I wish Daija would come.

"Why don't you invite her?" Amber says. I told her

earlier what happened between us. Most of the family has met Daija at one time or another.

"I already invited her. She's mad at me," I say.

"She was mad that day, but she's probably not anymore," Amber says.

"Then why didn't she come?" I know I sound like I'm seven, but come on.

Amber throws an arm around my shoulders and grins. She says, "Your girl didn't come because the last time she was here, she acted like a donkey, and now she's embarrassed. Text her and tell her I said get her butt over here."

Oh, Lord! I look around and see I have another situation to fix.

"Callie!" I say, waving her over to the trampoline from the patio. My aunties have her backed into a corner. She may never escape. "Aunties, can you excuse Callie, please?"

I shoot Daija a text, but she doesn't answer. Five minutes pass. I sigh. Callie squeezes my arm and says, "Give her time. She'll come around."

Grandma returns, side-eyes Amber, then laughs

as she hugs me. She pushes an envelope into my hand. "Happy birthday, sugar! I sure do appreciate y'all having your celebration before I leave for Africa. And besides..." She leans to whisper in my ear. "You know I couldn't leave the country without laying eyes on your sister."

I can't help laughing. "Yes, Gram, I know."

The gift-giving and cake-cutting are epic. Plenty of envelopes filled with cash, plus lots of other nice gifts.

Still no gift from Callie, though. When my uncles pass me their cards with cash inside, they pass a couple to Callie, too.

"We've missed a lot of her birthdays, gal, so don't go gettin' big-eyed about nothing," Uncle Arthur says to me. I hold my hands up.

"I didn't say a thing." I'm actually glad they included her. This whole faux birthday party for my gram's benefit feels a little weird. I'll be glad when all the attention is off me, and the parentals settle down with their old-school jams and grown-up cocktails.

Amber shouts, "Callie! Come on! We're going for a walk!"

I hug Mom and Daddy again for giving me a new iPad, then Daddy says, "Wait, there's one more."

He pulls out a tiny jewelry store bag and hands it to me. I open it to oohs and aahs.

"It's a bracelet," I say. "Real jewelry." It is so sparkly and perfect I can't believe it. I wave it to show everyone and get more oohs and aahs. Except from Taz, who's pointing his finger down his throat like he's gagging.

"Thank you, Daddy! Thanks, Mom!" I say.

Daddy, looking proud even though I'm sure Mom is the one who chose it, stands and shoos us away. "You and your sister and cousins, go for your walk! Go on! If Skipper arrives, I'll tell her how to find you."

The little kids are playing in Taz's fort and on the trampoline. Us bigger kids go for a walk.

We set off from our house. It's dusk, and the last dribbles of daylight are leaking from the sky, painting shadows across the neighborhood. I glance over at Callie, and she gives me a little smile.

We start telling my cousins about the competition between the camps and about the Sistahs Who Braid getting up in our faces.

I tell them, "Daija is mad because she says we should come up with a way to shut them down and shut them up!"

"She's right!" says Amber.

"I really think if we provide the better service, we'll come out on top. I really do!" I say.

Amber shakes her head and says, "You should've just slapped their faces and told them to sit down somewhere."

"Sure, assault is always the quickest route to conflict resolution—we learned about that in my civics class," Alana says dryly before rolling her eyes. "Shut up, Amber! Ain't nobody trying to catch a case!"

Everyone starts throwing around ideas of what to do next. Everything from offering free styles to doing TikToks.

"I...I have an idea," I finally say. Then I realize we're going right past the house where Angela, one of the Sistahs, lives.

Callie is still beside me. She looks at me, slips her hand into mine again, and gives it a squeeze. She flashes a small smile.

"Whatcha got, Mags?" says Alana.

"Pictures. Lots and lots of pictures. We need more flyers, more examples of our work. And more photos on Callie's Instagram, too." I turn to her, and her smile widens.

She says, "I am in charge of our account on Insta. We should post a lot of photos, as many as possible of new styles. We'll let everyone see how much better we are than them."

Alana says, "Are you sure you *are* better than them? I mean, no shade, but you really haven't seen what they can do yet. What if they're really good?"

Callie surprises me by speaking up. "Well, not to throw shade, but they have a lot of crooked parts and their kitchens are a bit cluttered, if you know what I mean."

Girl. I know what you mean. And nobody wants a "cluttered kitchen." That means the edges around the back of your head, where we tend to sweat, are messy. Real messy.

"I just wish we could get a lot of new style photos up right away," I say.

"Well, we've got a lot of heads right here," says Amber.

Then a voice I'm not expecting says, "And I'll help."

We all turn to find Daija.

"Hey," she says. "I got your texts."

The two of us are standing here eyeballing each other. I know she's not waiting for me to apologize to *her*, is she?

"Nice to see you could make it," I say, trying to keep the attitude out of my voice. I can feel the others staring. Amber being Amber, she can't help herself.

"Hey, chick!" she says, coming over and giving Daija a hug. "We're glad you could make it, girl. You and Maggie've been friends too long to be carrying on!" When I look at Daija, I can see that Amber is right. Even though I'm still feeling some kind of way, some of the tension between us fades. I don't want to stand around being pouty.

"I am glad you came, Daija," I say, meaning it. "Really."

She shrugs, looking at her feet. When she looks up, she has a shy smile that is so unlike her.

She says, "Me too."

Back at the house, we pull up Pinterest. Once we toss around our opinions, the tension between me and Daija lessens. But it doesn't completely go away.

While everyone is busy choosing styles, I pull Daija aside.

"So, are we going to be able to squash this and move ahead, for the good of the business?"

"I'm not the one who had a problem." She doesn't make direct eye contact.

"Really, Daija?"

When she turns back to me, at first, she looks as defiant as ever. I've got one hand on my hip, and she has her arms crossed.

Maybe it's because I'm not backing down, but she finally releases a long sigh, uncrosses her arms, then holds out a fist to bump.

"For the good of the business," she says.

That's when Amber squeals with delight after seeing the perfect style for herself.

"I'll do your hair," I say. Her hair is the same thick, soft texture as mine.

I take my time, sectioning her hair in front. She wants a wide cornrowed updo, which means working backward—you have to start at the nape of the neck and work upward. Then you decide how you want the front to look, whether the client wants the front even or circular, and when you're done you twist the braids into a pineapple atop her head. Not as complicated as it sounds, trust me.

I'm feeling a whole lot better—about a lot of things. About my party-not-party. About being able to make myself heard. About Daija.

Then I see Callie. She keeps glancing at the jewelry box with the new charm bracelet that Mom and Daddy gave me. When she looks up and our gazes meet, I see a sadness has crept into her eyes.

When we're in the driveway, saying farewell to the relatives, I whisper to her, "What's wrong?" Gram has us lined up for a hug line.

Callie shakes her head like nothing is wrong. When everyone is gone, it's just us and Daija. I'm talking to Daija about Braid Girls business like nothing ever happened. When I look around for Callie, however, I can't find her.

Why is she acting so strange?

❧ CHAPTER 15 ❧

Callie

I didn't give Maggie the bracelet I made for her.

No way could I give her my little homemade gift when her parents had given her something so lovely.

Once again, my feelings are a jumble. James and I have been getting closer, which I think is great.

But...

I still feel edgy, you know?

And that's nothing compared to how edgy we all are because of the no-good Sistahs Who Braid.

The morning is off to an awkward start. Daija

and Maggie still aren't back to their usual selves. We did a lot of hair and took a lot of photos at the party. Along with Amber and Alana, we also did two younger cousins, one boy and one girl, who'd been running around playing with Taz.

We have plenty of new pics and I put a lot online. I'll make more posters today. We ride to camp mostly in silence, and all I can do is hope the day will get better.

But then there are the emails. All cancellations from clients who'd made follow-up appointments. I think Daija might have an aneurysm. When Maggie emailed them back to ask if they need to reschedule, they all said the same thing:

"No, dear. The girls at Paradise say they can do it. And their prices are just a little bit cheaper!"

Then it gets worse.

We arrive at camp to find that not only have the Sistahs Who Braid put up banners on our side of the park, they are also holding signs that say things like "Honk if you love your hair!"

That afternoon, when we head back to our

braiding spot, in Mystic Cove (which doesn't feel mystical at all today), all of us are feeling pretty low.

And at least two of us—Daija and I—are feeling ready to fight back. Okay, I know I keep going back and forth between Daija and Maggie about who is right and who is wrong—but it's because part of me thinks they're both right.

I mean, Maggie is definitely right that we shouldn't be out front making a scene where the parents, campers, and other counselors can see us.

But Daija is also right that these so-called Sistahs are not the kind of girls who learn their lesson over time. We need to be loud!

Two clients are with Maggie and Daija. We have Daija's phone connected to a cordless speaker. Music plays, but none of us have much to say.

So, I drop onto the beach towel, tuck each foot on top of the opposite thigh, and try really hard to meditate away the negative thoughts.

I remind myself that things are going really well at the Wests' home. Our home. See, that's where things go wonky for me.

It's different when I think of their house as my house, too, instead of myself as some glorified visitor. However, when I start picturing myself as part of the West family…I don't know. It feels weird.

The most bizarre thing of all is, the happier I feel around them all, the guiltier I feel about feeling happy.

I've got a guilt bomb threatening to explode inside me any second. How can I la-di-dah off into the sunset with my shiny new family when my mom is…is gone?

Even thinking the words leaves me choked up and breathless.

Deep breath in.

Deep breath out.

My eyes shut and I repeat the mantra over and over inside my mind. My lip quivers as I try to make myself believe it.

I open my eyes and see that Keith has brought over two guys, both in need of some grooming. He's looking at Maggie with moony eyes, and she's avoiding eye contact in her adorably awkward way.

She is my sister. Plain and simple. We have a connection. I feel it. And I'm pretty sure she does, too.

Keith says, "So I have a way to help you with your business *and* get back at the Sistahs. Are you interested?"

Daija whips her head around so fast, she must've given herself whiplash. She says, "Boy! Spill it!"

And he does.

Suddenly, I'm not so deep in my feels anymore. I'm Callie Anderson, ready for action!

Keith's suggestion gives us a whole new way to fight back.

Operation Sugar and Spice and Sistahs with Lice— take one!

To get back at them for stealing our business idea, we're going to sneak over, take videos of the Sistahs and their bad braiding, and show why our braids and services are just plain better.

"Like a 'what not to do' kind of thing, right?" Daija says.

He nods. "And I could take some videos of you girls doing it the right way. You know, add it to your Instagram stories. Wouldn't that be cool?"

We agree, it would.

Maggie gets her cautious look. She doesn't want to tell us no, but she's not exactly down for more snooping. I can tell.

"Come on, Maggie! We have to do something! You know we do," Daija says, half-pleading, half-huffy.

Maggie frowns, seeming unsure of what to say.

Keith looks shyly in her direction, pushes his foot over to nudge her foot, and says, "It'll work. Trust me!"

The next day, we put the first part of our plan into action. Maggie is still super nervous, but I'm not. Not really. Being sneaky makes me feel like a spy. I love a good spy story.

We figure out how the Sistahs are sneaking back and forth into our campsite without being seen. They are coming across the thin strip of lake separating our camps.

Well, we have a canoe of our own over here. The plan is for me and Daija to sneak across while

Maggie stays with our campers, working on an afternoon craft. The others will be playing board games, watching movies, or reading.

Keith has told us where we need to be and when we need to be there. We synchronize our watches. No reason, really. It just sounds really cool.

At two thirty on the dot, Daija and I take off. Having never been in a canoe together, we need a little trial and error to find our rhythm. Daija snaps at me once, even though she's the one about to tip the boat. I keep silent, hoping she'll get herself right on her own. I don't want to end up in the lake.

Pretty soon, she manages to find her balance. I row us across, moving the paddles slowly so I don't make too many ripples. We luck out because it's kind of gray. Not stormy or misty, just a blah, gray day. Not the kind of afternoon when kids might be out or looking at the lake.

We reach the back shore, pull the canoe behind a nearby tree, then make for the door to their classroom building. It's exactly three o'clock. Keith is inside the slender door to let us in.

Now he looks a little scared. I feel it, too. Nerves.

When I glance over at Daija, she's wearing her determined expression. I swallow hard. Too late to back out.

"Follow me," Keith whispers. We do, tiptoeing down the hallway, stopping short at every scrape of a gym shoe or muffled conversation from some distant room. "Everyone is down in the multipurpose room. The Sistahs Who Braid are on the other side of the building. Outside. They found out you guys had a spot in the woods, so now they've done the same."

"Typical!" snaps Daija, immediately covering her mouth in fear she may have been too loud.

Both me and Keith go "*Shhh!*"

After a few more seconds, Daija stops again and whirls around. She narrows her eyes at Keith and says, "You're not setting us up, are you? Being a double agent so we get caught over here?"

Really, Daija?

Keith's long curls bounce furiously as he shakes his head. "No!" he whispers harshly. "I wouldn't do that to Maggie!" Soon as he realizes what he's said, his olive cheeks stain a bright pink.

"We believe you, Keith," I say, throwing a pointed look Daija's way. "Let's keep going."

He leads us down a back hallway. "We only use this hall in the mornings when we're setting up. The counselors and directors work mostly out of the front office, which is on the opposite side of where you guys came in."

When we get to the next hallway, the one that leads outside, Keith goes out first and looks around. The coast is clear, so we follow him down a path, winding through some woods.

My breath catches again, and I feel Daija stop short, too. There they are.

Lorilee is standing over a little girl in a lawn chair, pulling on her hair. The child is shrinking up and trying to pull away, but Lorilee is pulling back. Angela is sitting down, trying to work some cornrows. Only she can't seem to keep her parts straight. *Figures!*

She's not using the right moisturizer on the girl's hair. Too much oil. The hair is slippery but not hydrated.

Daija and I exchange a look. Keith whispers, beckoning us down behind a bush, saying, "If they see me, then see the videos on one of your stories, they'll suspect me. I'll get in trouble."

I nod. With his finger to his lips, Keith points to an area beside a bush that will give us enough cover to stay hidden, yet enough light to record what's going on.

"You've got fifteen minutes," he says, backing away. "I have to go back and show my face. I'll come back and get you, help you make it back to the canoe. Fifteen minutes, okay?"

"We hear you, chief," Daija says.

"Here we go," I say to Daija as Keith disappears into the trees.

"Here. We. Go!" Daija repeats.

We set up in the spot Keith showed us. He's right. It's the perfect cover. I aim my camera and begin recording. It would be comical, watching the Sistahs struggle with these girls' hair, if it wasn't so sad. To borrow a word from Cousin Amber, these "chicks" have stolen good clients, and they don't even know what to do with them.

"This is *soooo* great!" says Daija. "Look at that girl's hair, the one Angela is doing. Can't she see what's she's doing? That's no..."

She stops. A squirrel or something lopes through

the brush, making enough noise to draw their attention. Angela stands up.

"Who's over there?" she demands.

Daija and I freeze. If she comes this way, we're toast. I watch her client's face relax as she rubs her scalp where Angela has been trying over and over to part her hair. The little girl looks from Angela to Lorilee and says, "I'm telling my mama you hurt my head!"

That snatches Angela's attention back to her.

"No! You better not tell your mama. I *can* do your hair!" Arguing with her customer seems to have pulled her back to her task.

"We can't stay here much longer," I say, peering at the enlarged image of the hair tragedy taking place. Daija nods.

"I think I've got enough," I say.

She agrees. "Me too."

We back away, slowly...slowly...then *CRASH!* We step in a bed of twigs, dry and crackling.

"Told you somebody was out there!" We hear Angela's voice, but we don't stick around. We're running, hoping she's not right behind us. Soon as we clear the trees, we almost run smack into Keith.

"What's wrong?" he says.

"Gotta go! I think Angela is following us!" I say, barely stopping.

"I'll try to distract them," Keith calls after us. "Go!"

We scramble into the canoe as Keith races back toward the woods. My heart is racing a million miles an hour, and Daija hasn't blinked in minutes. Slow and steady, I push the water, urging my heart to slow down.

Maggie is waiting for us in the Heritage Park multipurpose room. Her expression is a mixture of relief and agitation.

"Did you get caught?" she asks.

Daija waggles her phone at Maggie.

"We made it. And you won't believe what we got!" I say.

CHAPTER 16

Daija

I'm glad Maggie didn't try to stop us. We had to do this!

Me and Callie upload the recording of the worst braiders in the Jacksonville area as soon as we get home.

Right away, we get tons of views. The two of us text back and forth for a long time. I don't hear from Maggie, though.

Still, I can't wait to see the look on Angela's face.

Maggie is being very formal and polite to me during the car ride to camp, which is her way of not picking a fight but not being happy, either. She is still hung up on the idea that we "don't need to focus on getting back at them, just worry about being *better* than them."

Well, that sounds good, but girls like Lorilee, Ciara, and definitely Angela won't learn their lesson that way.

The only way to teach them a lesson is by giving them a taste of their own medicine.

Even though I can't get Maggie to make eye contact, me and Callie keep glancing at each other. To borrow one of Callie's words, the "energy" in the car must feel different, because Kiki is throwing us looks, too.

"What's up with you girls this morning?" Kiki asks. The sound of her ticking blinker fills the car. A semi passes us and blows loose gravel onto the windshield. I flinch. Kiki narrows her gaze at me.

"Daija, what's gotten into you? You're jumpier than an understudy on opening night. You okay?"

Keeping my voice low, I say, "I'm fine, Kiki. It's all good. Really."

She doesn't believe me, but she doesn't say

anything else and turns into the parking lot. I breathe a whooshing sigh of relief.

Then, in her softest tone, as we're getting out, I hear Kiki murmur, "I hope you know you can come to me."

Kiki walks ahead of us, moving with purpose. Maybe that is where I get it from. I feel my muscles come alive with each step. I'm not worried about those Sistahs today. I can't wait to see their faces.

Everything is great, except...

"Maggie," I say as we walk away from the car, "are you still worried we'll get in trouble? Trust me, we're golden! This is exactly what they deserve."

"This is not how I want to do business. Not to mention, Daija, from the outset, I told you I wanted to do this so we could just have fun together. I told you at the beginning not to get too competitive. But...but..."

"What?" Okay, I do kinda raise my voice.

"Never mind!" she says, pushing past me, heading toward the building. Callie and I are left on the sidewalk. Maggie has never walked away from me like that.

"She isn't right, you know? About the whole father-daughter dance thing? I'm not just lashing out because deep down I feel sooo sad about knowing my father probably wouldn't be caught dead at a father-daughter dance with me. She's so, so wrong!"

I do my best to sound confident and all that, but even to me the words sound hollow.

Callie looks doubtful. "If you say so," she says. "But what if she's right? What if recording them, sneaking over there like that, what if it was a mistake?"

"Don't you go chicken on me, too!"

Callie turns around. "Maggie's not a chicken. She...she just thinks about things differently, that's all. And I'm definitely not chicken. I'm the one who actually recorded them, remember?"

"Look, Maggie is my best friend," I shoot back. "I've known her longer than you. And I say she'll be fine, okay?"

"If you say so," she says, sounding unconvinced.

It doesn't take long before the Sistahs arrive. Maybe it is petty, but I can't help myself. I wave and smile my sweetest, absolute best Tony Award–winning smile.

Angela looks like she might actually start growling, she is so mad. When I glance at Callie, I am thrilled to see she is enjoying their sour expressions as much as I am. I wish Maggie were out here to enjoy it, too.

"You think you're so funny, don't you?" Lorilee says. She stalks her way around the grassy circle to stand face-to-face with us.

"I don't know what you mean, Lorilee," I say, faking innocence.

Angela pushes her way between me and Lorilee, and I couldn't be happier to see her grimace.

She's all "That wasn't right. We saw what you posted on Instagram. You just caught us having a bad day. Those kids' hair was too tangled."

Lorilee and Ciara nod. Ciara adds, "And they were real tender-headed. That's not our fault."

I take out my phone and open the recording we edited. Not that Callie had to add anything—we actually had to cut it to fit into the format. We also have a version we made with comments and decals. I have it bookmarked ready to go. I turned the phone toward them.

"I don't know if the problem is just being

tender-headed," I say. "Looks like y'all having all kinds of problems."

Then I burst into laughter. Callie laughs, too, although hesitantly.

"Yeah, well, laugh now, 'cause we're going to get you back. So don't sleep on that!" Angela says with a flounce.

Callie and I put our heads together and wave goodbye.

I hit Replay over and over. I especially love the comments people leave.

> They're jacking up that girl's hair!
>
> Who told them they could braid?
>
> #badSistahs
>
> Don't let them near my head!
>
> What are they doing?

I know it's extreme, but we're battling for our dollars, okay?

I turn to find Callie looking at me. She says, "I'm not sure we should've done it. Maggie is still upset."

Coach Lori's whistle blows, and we rush across the lawn, leading the kids inside.

"Maggie'll be fine," I call over my shoulder to Callie, although I'm not really sure. "You'll see!"

I'm trying for another award-winning performance. But this time, my insides shake as I try to believe the words I'm saying.

The Sistahs are determined to get back at us after that, and they don't waste any time. Just before lunch, they strike while we're putting away supplies in the back closet.

"I still don't think it's right, pulling pranks and all that. It's..." Maggie pauses before saying, "Childish."

"Hand me the box," I say. I am on a stepladder. Callie passes me one of the boxes. Maggie doesn't look like her usual worried self; she looks ticked off. What is her deal?

I say, "Mags, we've got this. It's time those girls get a taste of their own medicine. They—"

I don't finish.

The lights go out. For several seconds, we freeze.

Callie asks, "A power surge?" The utility closet we're in is also where they keep the servers for the internet. I look over. The lights glow as green as always, twinkling in the dim stillness.

"No, can't be. The power is still on," I say. Slowly, I climb down from the ladder. Maggie automatically reaches up to help guide me down. Then it's like she realizes what she's doing and just as soon as I'm on solid ground, she snatches her hand away.

I'm about to ask her what her deal is when Callie hits the wall switch and the lights come back on.

"What's going on?" asks Maggie.

"I'm not sure," I say, reaching for the doorknob. When I go to twist the knob, it slips out of my hand. "*Ew!* Something gross is on the knob!"

I hold up my hand, showing the glop of something oily—possibly Vaseline. I feel my face tighten with anger.

"*Angela!*" I snarl.

"How'd they even get over here to lock us in?" Callie says.

"The same way we got to them!"

Maggie lets out another long sigh and says, "And

this is why I don't like pranks. It just goes on and on until it goes too far!"

I spin around, facing her. I've been trying to be nice. I'd actually been thinking about trying to see things her way. But she just won't let up. This is nothing if it means those videos we posted will get our customers to come back.

"Maggie, stop complaining and start helping!" Okay, maybe it comes out harsher than I meant it to. Still, I don't slow down. "I'm trying to save my business and my money!"

Callie, who is in the middle of texting Kiki so she'll come save us, pauses. Her eyes dart from me to Maggie.

Maggie scowls.

"Your business? Your money? Um, I think you've claimed credit for the Braid Girls so often, you're starting to think you really did come up with it all on your own. Well, news flash, Daija. You didn't!"

"Oh, so you're coming for me now? Is that how it is? My business, our business, whatever. You know what I mean." I feel my temper flaring up, feel the anger swirling in my belly, getting hotter and hotter.

"No matter who came up with it, you know you never would have done anything to make it happen if it weren't for me!"

That's the truth!

Maggie looks at me for a long time. So long that it starts to feel uncomfortable. She finally says, "You know, Daija, you've gotten so wrapped up in what the Braid Girls mean to you that it's keeping you from seeing what it could mean to all of us."

I snap, "What are you even talking about?"

"Those girls are loudmouths. Troublemakers. Don't let them get under your skin like that," she says. "This whole thing isn't about a business anymore. It's more like an obsession—an obsession with fighting just for the fight. Just because you're angry. Not because it's good business sense."

"Obsession!" I'm shrieking. I know I am. "Obsession? *Really?* You know what, Maggie? I think the real problem is, Angela might be right about one thing— you're a cowardly lion. Stop using your shyness or whatever as an excuse not to do something! Me and Callie are trying to fight back. When are you going to stand up for yourself? When are you going to stop being everybody's doormat!"

As soon as the words leave my mouth, I wish I could take them back.

Maggie gives me the hardest look ever. When Kiki opens the door, Maggie turns to walk away, but stops first. In a quiet voice she says, her eyes piercing into me, "Maybe it's time for me to start right now."

CHAPTER 17

Maggie

By Thursday, Daija and I still haven't said one word to each other. With each painful second that ticks by, I feel my summer of fun slipping away. And maybe our friendship, too.

Even the little clients whose parents happily rescued them from the Sistahs and sent them back to us can see things between us have been different.

"You think y'all so hot," Angela said to me earlier in the day. "We're going to get you back for putting up that video."

I was tired of all the drama. I looked at her and said, "Go ahead. I don't even care." That shut her up.

That's all bad enough.

But it gets worse. So, so much worse that afternoon.

I wonder if maybe I should try talking to Daija. Maybe. I still don't think I should apologize because I didn't do anything wrong. Not really. But being mad at each other is not helping either of us. I just want it to end.

We bring our lunch all week and eat together on the main lawn with the rest of the campers. Today we do the same, like usual. Only, the *unusual* part is that no one is talking until one of the little campers asks if my dad is coming to the dance.

I say, "I think so."

She grins shyly. "Mine is coming," she says. "We're dancing to a song by Beyoncé." After that, several kids pipe up about their mom or dad—who's coming and what music they're using. It puts me in a good mood. Good enough to think I can actually talk rationally to Daija.

So after lunch, I clear my throat and say, "We need to talk about how much we're planning to earn over the next few weeks. It's not nearly as much money as we did the first week. We're not picking up new customers or getting repeat customers at a good enough rate."

"Big surprise!" Daija says in a huff. "It's because of the Sistahs Who Braid!"

"Um, not really. I mean, yeah, they stole some of our clients, but over the past week, we really haven't done any promoting or anything, not like we did the first week or so. We really need to get back to that," I said.

But Daija just has to have one of her Daija moments. She balls up her sandwich wrapper, stands, and looks down at me. Then she says, "What we need is to find a way to shut them down for good!"

Then she marches off toward the classroom buildings.

After camp, I'm at home and ready to burst into tears. This is not how my summer is supposed to be. It's so awful. Daija doesn't plan to apologize, and neither do I. I'm so upset that when I go for a walk, I practically stalk around the neighborhood. I think I scared some little children with the smoke coming from my nostrils.

Later, at home, I feel calmer. I figure I can talk to Callie and get her opinion on what to do next, and we can go from there. It's funny how, without even realizing it, we've become close. At least, that's how it feels to me. I push open the door to our bedroom. It looks empty. However, when I go into my closet, I realize I can hear her voice from the bathroom. She sounds upset.

Then I hear something I wish I hadn't. It's Callie, and I think...I think she's talking about me!

"...can't take it anymore, Auntie...won't leave me alone. What? No, not really....Really? Well, she doesn't like me, and I don't like her, either...."

It's like getting punched in the chest. I'd thought at least *we* were good. Only, she clearly doesn't feel the same.

Is she really that miserable?

I leave our room for a while, then when it's my turn for the bathroom, I try to drown my sorrows in the shower. The water blasts me until it runs cold. I towel off, dress, and come back into our bedroom. I'm happy to see it's empty. I really can't face her yet. I slip out the patio door into the backyard. She never comes back here, and I really don't want to run into her.

I don't want to run into anyone.

At least, that's what I think until I walk around to the front porch and see someone moving up the walkway.

"Hey, I brought someone for you to meet," says my unexpected visitor.

"Keith! What are you doing here?" I ask. I am so relieved to see someone who isn't Callie or Daija.

"Someone wanted to meet you," he says again. A floppy-eared beagle sniffs the air. I bend and scratch his ears and the dog instantly begins licking my face. It's the best I've felt in days.

"Oh, thank you for introducing me to your doggy," I say.

"His name is Deku," he says.

My eyes widen. "Like Deku from *My Hero Academia!*"

"What do you know about anime?" Keith says. "That's one of my favorites!"

"Me too!"

We stand there staring at each other. The grin I feel spreading through me is a definite improvement to the gloom that's been following me.

"You and your girls seemed to have a weird vibe lately at camp," he says. He is so right. Today was the least fun day so far. "I thought maybe you could use a furry friend. Sorry you and Daija are feuding right now," he says.

I sigh. "It's not just Daija," I say. "You want to take a walk?" When he says yes, I text Mom and tell her I'm out walking the neighborhood with a friend. Then we take off before she can tell me not to.

"So what's up with y'all?" he asks. "You and Daija seem like you're not feeling each other at all!"

My shoulders slump. "I guess it's not just me and Daija. Seems like there's a problem with Callie, too. Only I don't know what the deal is." I tell him what I overheard. "I'm trying to be reasonable, you know, but I guess I expected more—from both of them. The whole business, our friendship, having a sister... everything, it's pretty much been a disaster."

He laughs when I make a face. I'm not trying to be funny. Not really. But I like making him laugh.

"I don't think it's a disaster," he says. "Y'all have to find a way to remember what brought you together in the first place."

"Not if what brought us together was circumstance and low self-esteem?" I reply. I begin telling him how I'd assumed that Callie wanted to be part of our family and wanted me as a sister, so I'd been trying hard to make that easier. "But maybe that's not what she wanted—ever!"

Then I tell him how I'm always coming up with ideas for things I want to do or try but never have the courage.

"Daija is right about one thing: The Braid Girls might've been my idea, but without her, I probably never would've made it happen."

We talk and talk some more. Saying everything out loud makes it feel less heavy. I blow out a long exhale and look for some of that "good energy" Callie's always talking about.

We reach the large playground and picnic area. Keith lets Deku off his leash.

"Aren't you worried he'll run off?" I ask.

"He's fine. We come here all the time, and it's safe for him. Let's sit over here," he says, pointing to a covered picnic table. When we sit, he goes on. "Okay, Maggie, let's break this down."

Keith runs through a list of questions: "What are you the most upset with Daija about? What are you most upset with Callie about? What do you want to do with the business? Have you discussed with them how you feel?"

"Wow!" I say, tickling Deku's ears after he trots over. "You're really good at this."

"My mom's a psychologist and my dad is a reporter. All they do is ask questions," he says, laughing. I think about how to answer his questions.

"I haven't discussed this with them, no. Daija and I both seem so angry with each other. And with Callie, I guess I'm really hurt. I thought things with us were good, but in that phone call she sounded so unhappy. It really hurt me."

"Sounds like you need to have a real conversation with them both. Maybe the conversation you overheard wasn't what you think," he says.

I give him a look. "Keith, I know what I heard."

"Do you?" he says. "Okay, maybe you do. But she could've been having a bad day, too. You said it happened today after you and Daija had another blowup. You can't know for sure if you don't talk to her."

I drop my head. He's right. Not just about Callie, either. Daija, too.

We get up and walk some more, this time talking more about his family than mine. "My little sister, Alejandra, is so sweet. We hang out and put puzzles together. We live right on the other side of the pool and clubhouse. Maybe you could come visit. Mom is always looking for someone to do Allie's hair."

We are strolling around the neighborhood when we cross the street and buy shaved ices.

"Your lips are blue," I say, feeling a blush creep across my cheeks. The electric blue ice has stained his tongue and lips.

"Well, yours are pink!" he says, laughing. Deku barks and Keith lets him have a lick of his shaved ice.

Up the street from the park, food trucks fill the intersection. We wander over to the carts, eyeing all the different foods. Still slurping our icy cones, we head toward a grassy spot. Keith says, "I...I think you're cool, you know?" He isn't looking at me. Not at all. Even in the shade, I see a blush creeping into his skin, too.

"Um...well, I mean you're pretty cool, too," I say, meaning it. We both sink to the grass. Enjoying the surroundings.

A question forms that I've been wanting to ask for days. I plunge ahead.

"Keith, why did you help us get that video on the Sistahs? Why'd you do it?" I ask softly.

This time, he looks directly at me.

"I did it because I didn't like what those girls were doing. It wasn't right, how they were acting. And I did it 'cause I felt bad for the little kids whose hair they were messing up. They don't know anything about braiding. I'm a better braider than they are, and I know I can't braid!"

"Goodness," I say, unable to hold down a laugh, "I didn't know you were so passionate about it."

After several moments of awkward silence, Keith gives me some dog biscuits, and we take turns letting

Deku jump for treats. Then Keith pushes his foot closer, touching my shoe with his.

"Now, back to what we were talking about before," he says, leaning back on his elbows and letting Deku lick his face. "You've got to tell them, Callie and Daija. You have to be real with them about what's up with you."

"Dealing with conflict isn't my greatest strength," I say, my voice going soft again.

"Don't think of it as a conflict," he says, sounding like the son of a therapist. "Think of it as conflict resolution."

CHAPTER 18

Callie

Maggie has been avoiding me for a few days. I'm not sure how her beef with Daija turned into a problem with me. But you don't have to be a seasoned spiritualist to sense she's been as cold to me as she's been to Daija. I have no idea why.

We are struggling through another breakfast. Tina and James West are trying to keep up the conversation for both of us, when Tina finally says:

"Okay, ladies, I'm not sure what's going on with you two, but fix it. You're bringing us all down and it's time to end it, whatever *IT* is!"

I look down like the secret of life is beneath the banana slices floating in my bowl of Cheerios. Then I hear Maggie clear her throat and speak up.

"Callie, Mom's right. I think we need to talk. I've already sent a text to Daija. She's coming over," she says. I think we're all a little surprised by her tone. It's bright and clear, not hesitant and uncertain. She sounds like a girl who knows what she has to say and is about to say it.

Good, because I've got something to say, too.

I've been thinking. As much as I want to fit in, I never meant to make Maggie feel uncomfortable in her own home. I spoke with Aunt Lana a few times. She's willing to let me travel with her if I want.

It's not what I want, of course, but maybe this isn't the right time for me to be here. At least, not yet.

"Bloop-bloop-bloop!" Taz growls.

"Are you in attack mode, little buddy?" I ask.

"The aliens are tired of you ignoring each other. It. Is. Time. For. Battle." He puffs out his cheeks and gives us a deep scowl. He looks menacing, or as menacing as a growling seven-year-old can look.

Maggie reaches over and pokes his cheeks, letting

the air out. She says, "It. Is. Time. For. You. To. Scrape. The. Dishes. Bloop-bloop-bloop!"

Everyone laughs.

A few minutes later, Daija arrives. The three of us go to Maggie's room. Daija looks sullen, like she doesn't want to be bothered. We still haven't gone to ballet together since she invited me. The time for that hasn't been right, either, I guess.

"We need to talk," Maggie says. Unlike this entire week, she's not frowning when she says it. She has her clipboard and a pen, and she is wearing a very un-Maggie-like white T-shirt with denim shorts.

Business casual if you're in middle school.

"Are you going to yell at me and call me unprofessional again?" says Daija, arms crossed.

I take a breath. Uh-oh. We're not getting off to a good start. Maggie lets out a breath, but she doesn't look put out or bothered.

"No yelling," she says. "Discussing."

She clears her throat again, then takes a moment to look us both in our eyes.

She says, "The past week or so hasn't been our best." Daija makes a rude snort. Maggie ignores it. "If we're going to make this business work through this summer and beyond, we're going to have to learn how to talk to one another."

"I have been...," Daija begins, head on an instant swivel before Maggie gives her the hand.

"No, no, Daija. We're all going to get a chance to speak. I want to know how you're feeling and how to avoid creating these same problems in the future. But first, if I may, let me tell you my issue."

Again, she pauses, looks from me to Daija, then goes on:

"My issue is that I am very cautious. I am also very blessed. Being cautious makes me take my time and consider everything. Being blessed means that I'm fortunate enough to have parents who can pay for the things I'm interested in, so that my business money is for extras, not for something I really love, like ballet lessons.

"Daija, I'm so sorry that I didn't try to better understand what you needed," Maggie says. "I was all about having fun and trying to learn business skills. As a business, I was totally taking it seriously, yet I didn't really appreciate how serious it all was to you. I am so sorry."

I can't help grinning wide at Maggie. *Well said, sister!*

Daija's mouth drops open and her skeptical attitude melts away. She moves toward Maggie, as though to wrap her in a hug, but Maggie, sitting crisscross on the bed, pulls away.

"But Daija, if you ever call me a 'doormat' again, girlfriend, you and I are going to have a Come to Jesus meeting. I'm not your doormat, or anybody else's, okay?"

Daija puffs up like she's about to clap back, then it's like all the hot air squeezes out. She looks down at her feet.

"Maggie," she says, "I'm sorry, too. Really sorry. I never should have said that to you. I was...feeling overwhelmed, I guess. And I'm sorry about ever pranking those Sistahs. You said it would only lead to more pranks. I got so caught up in the back and forth, I lost sight of our primary goals—making money and spending time together as friends."

They reach for each other and hug. I'm so touched that I'm the one who starts crying.

"Callie, why're you crying?" Maggie asks.

"It's so touching. I hated seeing you mad at each other. It was totally bad for your karma."

Maggie laughs, saying, "And I know things between me and you have been shaky, as well. But after overhearing you on the phone, I felt hurt. I mean, I didn't know you were so unhappy here."

"What do you mean?" I ask.

"You were on the phone with your aunt and saying something about how you can't take it anymore and how someone won't leave you alone. Then I heard you say, 'She doesn't like me, and I don't like her, either.' So I figured you were talking about me. About us."

Where'd she get an idea like that?

"When did you hear me say that?" I ask.

"A few days ago. Right here in the bedroom. You were in the bathroom, and I could hear you on the phone. I guess you didn't know I was in here," she says sheepishly.

It takes a few seconds before the answer comes to me:

"Grandmother!"

"Our grandmother?" Maggie frowns, looking over at Daija.

"No," I say. "My grandmother in Nassau. She and I don't get along. She called me a few days after I got here and told me that my moving here made her look bad to her friends. She said I needed to come back to the islands. When I told her no, she got upset. I was telling Aunt Lana that I didn't care if she was mad because she doesn't like me either."

Maggie made a circle with her lips and said, "Ooooh!"

"And I don't want to leave. I was only thinking about it because I didn't want you to feel like I was trying to push you out of your own house."

"We've been real knuckleheads!" Maggie says.

Daija, whose head has been swiveling back and forth like a spectator at a tennis match, laughs. She says, "The realest!"

Before she can say more, the door to Maggie's room opens and our father steps inside.

His voice rumbles even though he's speaking softly. "So, have you girls worked out your differences?"

I look at Maggie, who nods, so I nod, too.

He says, "I got a call last night from your Aunt Lana. She says you're thinking about leaving us?"

"Not anymore. Not that I ever was, not really!" My voice gets high and squeaky.

"It's okay, Daddy, we're working it all out," Maggie says.

"Yeah, Mr. West," says Daija. "We're fixing everything."

He sighs deep in his chest and says, "I'm not sure what any of that means, but..." He turns to me: "Calliope Anderson-West—yes, I said West, because that's how I think of you—my wife tells me conflict among teen girls is normal. It might be normal, but it's not common for people to try to up and leave their families.

"Listen, I don't care what else is going on. From now on, you two have to understand we are all family. I know Aunt Lana is family, too. But, baby, you're my little girl. Okay, my not-so-little girl. And you guys are sisters. Not this 'half sister' nonsense. You're sisters. Deal with it. You're going to have disagreements. Fine. But the answer is to work them out. This is home now, Callie. You are home."

He turns and leaves without another word. I look at Maggie, feeling tears brimming in my eyes.

"Papa West got deep on us, didn't he?" says Daija. Maggie laughs. I feel wired, like I've been hooked up to a battery. My skin is vibrating. That's a lot to take in.

It's the feeling of being home.

CHAPTER 19

Daija

There's no camp today or for the rest of the week because of the Fourth of July holiday.

After talking over the weekend, we all agree to be better at speaking up about what we need and want.

And we agree to do a better job of checking our egos and our emotions. A lot of upset could have been avoided, but hey, as Kiki said, we're twelve. Sometimes, we just gotta learn the hard way. After we all got everything out in the open, we styled one another's hair. We talked the Braid Girls business, but we also just talked.

Hanging out and not feeling so tense was a good thing.

On Monday, it is time to let my toes do the talking. The studio is super warm and the air smells like dust and chalk. Miss Honey looks up as we cross the honey-blond wood floors. I am not alone.

"Miss Honey, this is Callie. My friend."

"Nice to make your acquaintance, Miss Callie. Come on show me what you can do!" After that, it's game on.

Truth is, from what I've seen, she's all right. And it's clear Maggie has gotten stronger since having her around.

A few weeks ago, admitting that would have hurt more. Now I realize there's enough love and friend-ship to go around.

"You're doing a good job, Callie, especially for someone who has been away from dance for so long," I hear Miss Honey say. She has her hand on Callie's back and is watching her form. Even though I'd already invited her, I'd felt hesitant about bringing her with me because, well, I was afraid she'd show me up.

Now, watching her, I realize every time Miss Honey gives her a compliment or criticism, it helps me, too.

For two hours, we go through a series of moves designed to strengthen our calves, increase flexibility through our feet, and increase confidence when we're on the tips of our toes.

"You've got three weeks, Daija, before your audition. How are you feeling?" Miss Honey asks at the end of our workout.

I'm sitting in a pool of sweat. My heart is pounding, and my feet crackle when I rotate my ankles. I take a swig from my water bottle and catch my breath.

"Better," I finally answer. "Still nervous, though."

"You have improved a lot. Catch your breath," Miss Honey says, "and meet me at the barre."

She does this sometimes. After the workout, she has me do lifts onto my toes before my muscles cool down. Callie is sitting beside me. She looks like she's been beat up. Her skin is blotchy with sweat and the heat of blood circulating rapidly through her veins.

I move as gracefully as I can toward Miss Honey.

My shoulders are back and my body is centered. With light fingers, I rest my hands on the barre. My feet are in second position. I sweep one foot outward, flex it, and do two quick kicks to the side.

Then I turn to face the wall. Holding my body in alignment, I feel myself breathing.

My mind blocks out all images of anyone else, and I can only feel the movement of my body, hear the music move from the speakers to my heart and travel through my muscles.

I bend my knees, plié. And lift, and...

I'm on my toes.

Not wobbling. Not holding my breath.

I am en pointe!

CHAPTER 20

Maggie

On my actual birthday, Mom and Daddy plan to take us to watch fireworks aboard a naval warship. That thing is huge.

With camp closed for the week, and no clients, we style and restyle one another's hair.

Callie talks me into knotless box braids that curl at the ends, I put Daija's hair in twists, and Daija puts Callie's hair up for a change. We are all feeling super chic.

We still have time to make our business a super-success and standout from any competition. And by "competition," you know I'm talking about the Sistahs with No Style.

Mom and I are in the kitchen packing up picnic foods that we'll eat on the ship's deck—Southern-style potato salad, fried chicken wings, bright red watermelon slices, a cooler of sodas.

Somewhere between packing the orange soda and helping to dredge the chicken for the perfect coloring, I turn to Mom and blurt out, "Mom, did you get ticked off when you found out about Callie? I mean, if you did, I'm glad it didn't last too long. I'm glad she's here. You know?"

She laughs a little. "You're a good sister, Maggie. I knew the minute I heard about her that I wanted you girls and Taz to have a chance to meet and be a family. But I also wanted it for your father. He had no idea about her. None. After he found out, it was eating him up. He was really mad at Clover for a while, although he didn't like to show it."

"But you still didn't answer my question," I say. Now we're wrapping aluminum foil around ham and cheese sandwiches. "Were you mad at all?"

Mom thinks for a moment. "Um..." She frowns,

※ 225

like she's really giving it a lot of thought, then says, "Not mad. More shocked than anything else. I know your father. His sense of responsibility, honor, all that. I know how he is. Finding out almost thirteen years later that Callie existed without him knowing, that was a big deal. For me, I was more of the mindset that she's family now. Let's make it happen."

"Mom," I say, leaning into her, "you're amazing."

"Thanks, honey."

We finish stuffing the picnic baskets and I grab an extra blanket.

Mom drops an arm over my shoulders. "I know this is a lot to absorb all at once, but, baby, you're getting a chance at something amazing. The chance to have a sister."

"Yeah, Mom," I say, boosting the big basket onto my hip. "We sisters are the best."

"Time is running out for camp," I say. We're aboard the naval vessel, spending some time chatting before the fireworks. "If we want to build our reputation back up and nail down a list of repeat clients before school starts, we have to work fast."

Callie says, "And we have to stay positive."

Since our talk, I'm feeling like the girls and I understand one another better. We had been holding on to our feelings, not really letting one another in. Clearing the air lifted a ton of weight off all our shoulders. After all, if I could stand up to Angela Cook, surely I could talk to my own friends.

I say, "I have some ideas for advertising and boosting the business. Keith and I were talking about it...."

"You mean when you were out 'walking his dog?'" Callie uses air quotes.

Oh, honestly!

"Don't use air quotes. We did walk his dog," I say.

Callie and Daija exchange looks, then they break into howls of laughter. Daija adds, "That's right! Tell her, Mags. You're really, really just 'dog walking,' and not at all gazing into his eyes for hours and hours."

I swing at her, playfully of course, but she ducks.

"Shut up, Daija!" I say, lifting one eyebrow. "Anyway, like I was saying...I have some ideas."

"I'll bet Keith has some ideas, too," Callie says.

And they're laughing at me. Again.

Okay, maybe this isn't the best time to talk business, anyway. I lie back against the lawn chair and stare out over the water.

A velvet sky hangs overhead like warm yarn, cozy and soft, reaching across the heavens. The navy blue beyond sparkles like a military procession decked out in medals. Only with more *boom!*

Taz sits between Callie and me, holding both our hands in his. Something about the setting—being aboard the ship, looking out over the water—feels like Honshu, Japan. Despite my negative feelings about living there, it was a very beautiful place.

Only now, instead of instantly feeling the pain and negativity that always go along with memories of Japan, I see the horizon, alight with flashing crayon colors of light. And my mind can picture the mountains that would have been in the distance if we were in Japan.

I can picture the beauty of the place that once had meant pain and ugliness to me. Fireworks explode, erupting in light that outshines the monsters of my past.

And it's beautiful.

CHAPTER 21

Callie

Tell me what my mother was like when you knew her," I say.

I'm at the shipyard with James. It's the day after the fireworks. He brought me on base with him to show me around, something he's done with Taz and Maggie plenty of times.

It's my turn now.

Last night, when we got back from the Fourth of July celebration, Maggie pulled me aside. She said, "I'm tired of watching you tiptoe around him. Tell him you want to talk!"

"When did you get so bossy?" I asked her.

Her smarty-pants answer was "Oh, I've always been bossy. Now I'm just speaking up so more people know it!"

I'm aboard a naval ship for the second day in a row. Only, this time, I'm standing at the railing beside the man I've dreamed about longer than I can remember.

He still feels like a stranger. But he's a stranger I'm slowly getting to know.

"Clover," he says, smiling lightly behind his mirrored lenses. "Clover was so different from any person I'd ever met...."

He tells me that Mom liked the same music back then, and he was fascinated by how different they were from each other.

I wave a fly away from me, squinting up at him in the bright sun. "Here," he says, taking an extra pair of sunglasses from his pocket. "Put these on.

"Clover was all about good vibes and good energy; I was a Florida boy who believed in hard work, not chakras and crystals. She fascinated me."

I ask, "Did you love her?" I'm frowning, looking up at him.

"Are you all right?" he asks. I nod quickly.

He goes on, saying he cared about her very much. They only dated for about two months. A summer romance. "I was working on a friend's father's fishing boat out of Abaco. She and I, we met at the beach."

Now we're walking along the deck. It's a beautiful Florida day. Sunlight slashes across the water, bouncing back to our sunglasses. A few sailor guys pass us, and even though James is not wearing a uniform, he snaps off a salute.

"Did you like being in the navy?"

"I did."

"Maggie thinks you regret not reenlisting, and she feels guilty about it."

He stops midstride, turns, and looks down at me. "Seriously?"

I nod again. "Seriously. She...I don't know what happened in Japan, not the details. She'll only refer to it as the incident. Except, I think she did sort of mention kicking some kid in his..."

I feel my face redden as I realize what I almost said.

He laughs.

"So, all I know is she still feels like you left the navy before you were ready."

My image reflects back to me off his lenses. I see my thin braids—done by Maggie—whipping around behind me. Wind on the water this morning is moving quickly. I'm not sure what I am expecting, but I definitely don't expect him to break into laughter all over again.

"Maggie is wrong about that," he says. We reach a railing and begin going down a narrow metal staircase. He automatically places his hand on my back, guiding me down the steps. When we reach ground level, he snaps a salute at a few more sailors and we walk down to the water's edge.

"I'll talk to Maggie. Tina was tired of being a navy wife. I think she had a harder time overseas than Maggie. She says she never felt accepted. She didn't get along with the administrator at the school where she was working. That whole situation was a mess. When Maggie had her run-in with those kids,

Tina said she was done. And that was all there was to it."

We had stopped, but now we're moving again. Sea birds screech above the water, dipping and swooping across the sky.

Then I get the courage to ask the question I've wanted to ask since I first laid eyes on him.

"Were you...you, um...Did you get mad when Mom called you? When you found out about me?"

When he nods, I feel my heart sink all the way into my kneecaps.

"Yeah, I was pretty upset," he says. I can barely hear him because my whole body has gone numb. All that stuff he said back at the house last week, about us being family. Did he really mean it?

He goes on. "She had no right, keeping a child from me like that. She never gave me a chance."

"Huh?" I say, only half-hearing him.

"Well," he says, looking curiously at me, "you asked if I was upset when I learned about you and I said yes. Your mom should have told me when she was pregnant."

"Would you have married her?" The question

jumps out of me. I slap my hand over my mouth, but it's too late. It's already out there.

"I doubt it," he says. "We weren't in love, and we both knew it. Besides, I don't think Clover ever wanted to get married. She told me that more than once that summer. I remember that. Remember thinking how that was just another way she was different from other girls I knew."

I agree with him about Mom. "I think you're right about her not wanting to get married. I never remember her saying anything about wishing she had a husband or anything like that."

He nods. "I love being married. And I love being a dad. And when I heard about you...I knew right away that I'd love you, too."

The feelings I've been pushing away come flooding out. I throw my arms around his waist and start bawling my eyes out, blubbering the whole time about—everything.

I tell him how much I always wanted to know who my father was, and about how hard Mom fought against ever telling me.

Then I get into the things that have been

bothering me since I came to Tangerine Bay. How every time I feel myself getting settled with the family, I feel disloyal to Mom somehow.

"Just like Maggie feels guilty about you leaving the navy, I feel like...like maybe, if I'd been nicer to Mom, if I could've been more supportive, maybe she wouldn't have gotten so stressed out. And maybe she'd still be alive!"

I feel his chin rest on the top of my head, feel his arms tighten around me as my whole body shakes with sobs.

"*Shh, shh, shh,*" he repeats again and again. I can't even see through my own tears, which is good, because I'd hate to see the expressions of the people around us.

After a while, I shudder out the last of my tears.

"Feel better?" he asks, handing me a handkerchief.

"Yes," I answer, sniffling. "I think so."

We walk for a while in silence. Crushed white shale and pebbles form gravel in the parking lot. An old oil drum is lined with a toxic green trash bag, and a snowy white plover is sitting on the can's rim.

James doesn't speak until we're back inside the car. He cranks the engine, then the A/C, but he doesn't drive away.

Instead, he sits there, looking straight ahead through the front window for a while, gathering his thoughts, I guess.

Finally, he turns to me and says, "You know none of that is your fault, right? Kids rebel. If rebelling kids was fatal to parents, there wouldn't be a mom or dad left walking the earth. You haven't done anything wrong."

My voice is small, but it holds a note of pleading. "I just wish I knew why she wouldn't talk to me about you. Knowing I'll never have that answer... sometimes it's just painful."

"I thought you were at peace? That you were so involved with your mantras and yoga?" he says. When I look at him, he has a sly grin. He's teasing me a little. I give him a shove in the side, the way I've seen Maggie do a hundred times.

"Yeah, okay, I am trying to be more zen, more centered. But sometimes, I'm doing it more out of a tribute to Mom than because of anything I get from it."

"Do you get anything from it? Far as I know, Clover was always like that."

I sigh. "I dunno. Maybe. I started getting more into it after she got sick. I'd meditate with her. I hadn't done that in a long time." My voice dips a little. "Sometimes, yeah, I guess the mantras make sense. And sometimes I wish I knew how to box so I could punch through a wall!"

James barks out a laugh and says, "I can help with that." He looks over at me, reaches out, and touches my hand. "Callie, whatever it takes to get through this grieving, I...we're here for you. Honestly, I saw how happy you seemed—and 'centered,' to use Clover's word—and I thought you were handling things very well. Tina, on the other hand, wasn't so fooled."

"I thought if I showed up being all sad or whatever, you guys might not want me around as much. Who needs a sad e-girl?"

He frowns, squinting at me. "An 'e' girl? What in the world is that?"

"An e-girl, you know, like an emotional girl."

"Sorry if I'm not up on all the hip new language, know what I mean?" he says. He does some really old pop and lock move with his arms from like a hundred years ago. He is so corny. I feel like I've loved him forever.

That doesn't stop me from groaning from his utter dadness. "Oh, so you've got jokes?" I say. "Thanks...*Dad*."

For the rest of the day, I call him Dad about a zillion times. By bedtime, everyone in the house is playfully mocking me. I don't care. He's my dad. And I love him, too.

Later that night, as I drift off to sleep, a coolness as sweet as midnight swirls off the ocean then rushes through me. Then a fluttery feeling, like butterfly wings against my cheek, tickles my insides.

It's the same feeling I had back at the seafood restaurant not long after I got here. The feeling, the scent...

Mom.

I can't prove it. But somehow, I know it's her. Letting me go. Letting me fly.

Now, eyes grainy, heart light, I recite my own mantra:

I am home. I am home. I am home.

CHAPTER 22

Daija

Kiki always says, "God don't like ugly hearts!"

Too bad nobody told the Sistahs Who Braid. After writing bad comments on our photos online and stealing our customers, they quickly go out of business.

Not because they are the worst—which they are—but because they are terrible braiders!

Now, ask me if I am sad:

You know I am not!

Of course, when camp starts back and the campers return, the same parents who deserted us for the

Sistahs return. Maggie pinches me and says, "You better not say 'I told you so' to these parents."

Regardless of the Sistahs going down in flames and us having more business than ever, we have to face a week filled with crafts, activities, and rainstorms—repeat!

Callie joins me the next day for a ballet class. I have to admit, it is nice having her here. Miss Honey is impressed with Callie's technique, which makes me want to see what she's doing so I can do it better.

"It's been good practicing with you," I admit to her when our class ends.

"Thanks," she says. "I loved ballet when I was in it, but I'll admit, it's hard getting back in shape the way I used to be."

"You'll get there," I say encouragingly. And I mean it. If she sticks with it, I know she really will.

It is the last week of camp, and all of a sudden, everything is moving in hyper-speed. Despite all the positive steps we've made as Braid Girls and as friends, there's one thing we've been totally silent about:

Me inviting my father to this little father-daughter dance.

We're having a sort of show-and-tell before the dance. Parents will be invited to come and see their kids' work. We'll serve iced tea, lemonade, cookies, and cake. And afterward, we'll have the dance.

Finally, Maggie asks, "Did you ask your father?"

We're arranging the kids' best crafts on a table underneath the pavilion. I shake my head.

"Nope," I say. My voice drops, then I blow out a sigh. "He'd just say no."

That evening when I get home, I go right into my stretches. Kiki is cooking dinner and the smells are swirling around everywhere. I am inhaling the warm, spicy scents when I hear the doorbell.

We don't get a lot of drop-ins.

Kiki goes to the door. I hear another voice. Male. I can't make it out at first. Then:

"Daija!" Kiki yells.

Who is it?

I rush out, down the hall, down the townhouse stairs, and into the living room.

"Dad? What's going on?"

My father is sitting on the sofa. Kiki hands him a tiny cup of the extra strong Cuban coffee he loves so much. He stands when I enter the room.

"Ah, Daija, how good it is to see my beautiful daughter again!" he says.

"Well, you're so busy," I say with as little attitude as possible.

He takes a sip of his coffee. "Thank you, Kiki," he says, lifting the tiny cup toward her, "as always, this is excellent."

She gives him a look, and I know instantly that she must've called him. Normally, I'd get annoyed with Kiki for interfering. However, this time, I let myself smile inside. Since standing me up in June, then bringing my brothers over for me and my friends to do their hair, we haven't really hung out at all.

"I have to check on dinner," Kiki says before leaving the room. My father and I exchange looks. Soon as she's back in the kitchen, the two of us laugh.

"Is this what a setup feels like?" I ask. I'm trying to keep it casual, you know? Like I'm not trying to be all needy.

But then I think, you know what, I'm twelve. And a twelve-year-old is allowed to be needy once in a while where her parents are concerned.

He reaches his arms out for me, and I let myself be folded into his hug. "I am so, so sorry for neglecting you these past weeks. I have had the same talk with the boys. And my wife. I am afraid that moving my law practice has been much more difficult than I'd imagined a few months ago. Please have patience. I promise, it will get better for all of us."

I feel speechless.

My father is always telling me he's busy. I guess I thought he somehow made time for his other family. It's never occurred to me that they are missing him almost as much as I do.

"It's okay," I finally say.

"No, no, no, it is not okay. One of the reasons me and Alicia chose to move up here was so that I could be closer to you. Did you know that?"

I shake my head. "No," I say. "I didn't."

We talk. I feel nervous telling him about ballet, but I do it anyway. "I...I'm really working hard as a dancer, Daddy. I want..."

Kiki, leaning against the doorway with her arms crossed, says, "They're having a father-daughter dance. It would take about an hour out of your schedule on Thursday. Last day of camp. You should come."

Before I can gasp and say "Kiki!" she is gone again.

"You'd want me to come to something like that?" he says, turning back to me.

I shrug, going for nonchalance. "If you want to. I mean, Maggie's dad is going to be there with her and Callie. Anyway, um..."

A braid falls loose and I automatically start twirling it nervously around my finger. I've seen Maggie do that, too. It's a braid thing.

He shrugs, smiles.

"I think I can make it."

No words will explain the beam of happiness bubbling inside me. Before I lose my nerve, I add, "We'll need a song."

Suddenly, my father looks alarmed. He says, "I don't have to do ballet, do I?"

I burst out laughing.

"No. Just regular dancing."

"Okay, we'll play our song," he says.

"What song?"

"You know, when you were little, you loved that one song. I used to sing it to you."

Now I'm really frowning. What in the world? Then the most unbelievable thing happens. My father, still wearing his fancy lawyer suit and starched white shirt, not to mention his silk tie, starts rapping.

Kiki has come back and is standing there looking at him, laughing and shaking her head. She looks at me and says, "When you were learning to walk, he'd play that song and you'd practically run around the house."

For the next ten minutes, we cry so hard from laughing.

It feels just like old times.

CHAPTER 23

Maggie

All week, kids have been going cuckoo bananas. And we've been swamped with business. It's looking like come the school year, we're going to have more repeat customers than we know what to do with.

Now that we've gotten all set up for the show-and-tell fair, I can't wait to get this day over with. We're near the lake between Paradise and Heritage Parks. Rows and rows of tables are set up to display arts and crafts; others are filled with platters of cookies and juice and a huge sheet cake.

I'm in love with the jewelry table. Callie worked with a group of kids who could handle the smaller beads and wire. The bracelets she helped them make are stunning.

"Your jewelry is amazing," I say, eyeing several pieces on the table. One piece stands out to me. It has clear beads, white beads, and aquamarine-colored beads mixed in, along with tiny seashells on it. It would be like having the beach on your wrist.

"I really like this one," I say, pointing to it.

"Really?"

"Yeah, it looks so island chic."

What she says next surprises me. "I made it for you," she says, her voice almost a whisper. "For your birthday."

"Then why are you selling my gift?" I ask, hands on my hips. "You can't go around selling someone's gift before giving it to them. That's not right."

She picks it up, letting the links dip between her fingers. The sunlight makes the beads glow.

"I was going to give it to you at your party...then I saw the beautiful bracelet your dad gave you. It was so amazing, and I felt like, well..."

"Give me that!" I say, reaching over and gathering the delicate piece of jewelry into my hand. "I'm not even listening to that nonsense. That's my bracelet now."

We pause, then I hug her sincerely and say, "Bloop-bloop-bloop! That means thank you."

The day goes by fast and before I know it, I see Daddy. Is that a...

Boombox?

Will that thing even play? Quickly, I run over to Callie and say, "Girl, if you know what's good for you, you better run. Daddy's been riding in his way-back machine and thinks it's 1985!"

But instead of running away, like I plan to do, Callie runs directly toward him. "Dad!" she calls out, proudly. She calls him Dad about a zillion times a day now.

As much as I want to run and hide, I see Coach Lori heading to the microphone, gathering parents and campers and everybody under the tent. There's a DJ and everything. Daddy goes over and says something to the DJ, who looks almost as old as Dad.

This can't be good.

Coach Lori thanks everyone for the participation and for making the session run so smoothly. I cut my eyes across the way at the Paradise Park kids. Keith waves, and I wave back. Then I feel someone tap my elbow.

"Ciara?" I say, surprised.

The same Ciara who is a Paradise Park junior counselor and former braiding rival.

"Oh...uh, I mean, hey, Ciara. What's up?" I can't help it. The eyebrow lifts all on its own. My eyebrow has trust issues.

"Hey, Maggie," she says. She's not with her posse today. What is she about to do? Are Lorilee and Angela going to jump out of someplace?

"I wanted to say, um, sorry about everything. Angela, well, you know how she is. I wanted to know if you'd be okay with me making an appointment."

"An appointment?" I lower my voice and try to sound more like a young professional. "I mean, an appointment to get your hair braided?"

She nods, looking slightly embarrassed. She says, "See, the whole thing with the Sistahs Who Braid started as a prank. We knew we couldn't really braid, not like you guys. Just, one thing led to another, and..."

"It got out of hand," I say, finishing her thought.

She nods. "Most definitely got out of hand." I tell her I'd be happy to do her hair, and when she leaves, I can't wait to tell the girls all about it!

Then the music starts. A familiar, old-school song starts to play. A nineties male R&B singer belts out the song's intro.

Then the beat drops and as I look around, it's like night of the living dead. Parents, even grandparents, are bumping their shoulders around, swaying to the beat, smiling. Tragic.

But that's not even the worst part.

Oh, no!

The worst part is when out of nowhere, Daddy and Callie take center stage. They have created a routine.

Quick! I drop down and hide beneath a table of cookies. All I see are feet. Then I feel someone dragging me out of there.

"Mom! Don't make me look! Don't make me!" I

beg. I try burying my face in her shoulder, but she's not having it.

"If I've gotta look, and Taz has to look, you have to look, too!" she says.

"But...do they know people can see them?" I ask, cringing as I see Callie and Daddy attempting to do something called popping and locking.

"You better be glad Callie is here," Mom adds, "or that could be you out there. He's already sensitive over the fact you wouldn't dance with him."

"I'll dance with him at home as much as he wants. As long as no one can see us. *Ever!*"

Finally, mercifully, the song ends. The grownups are all on their feet, clapping to the beat, then applauding.

Mom not only applauds, she whistles. Taz looks over at me and whispers, "Maggie, I'm with you this time. Glad I don't see none of my friends!"

"Bloopity-bloopity-bloop to that," I say, giving the little dude a fist bump.

Daddy and Callie join us, and all I can do is shake my head while Mom proudly applauds him and tells him what a good dancer he is. I guess that's what love is—white lies in the face of really bad dancing.

After several more performances, everyone is on the dance floor. That's when I notice Daija. And her father.

Daija looks like she's having the time of her life. And when the song ends, her father twirls her around the floor. They look really good together.

Really, really good.

Then it hits me—a summer of fun doesn't work unless the people around you are truly enjoying themselves, too. I can see that now. And it makes me happy.

CHAPTER 24

Daija

I about bust out of my dress trying to keep from laughing at Callie and Mr. West.

"Thank you for choosing a more, um, dignified style of dance," says my father. Even though we talked about dancing to the old rap song from when I was a kid, I instead chose something a little more classy. I am dressed in my ballet costume. He steps back and holds up my hand, allowing me to twirl.

"Dad," I say before he pulls me back, "thank you for being here. Thank you so much."

I prance around—en pointe—showing off my form.

Dad and I practiced. It is only a minute-and-a-half piece. He basically has to guide me while I do what I do. It's not a complicated deal, and it's not dazzling.

But I couldn't be happier. ◆

The music ends and there is applause. The Wests are hooting and hollering. I slip my arm through my father's. He looks amazing in his tailored black suit. Very chic.

We walk toward Maggie and her family, our arms linked. My dad moves his hand to my back to guide me as we approach.

"James, how are you?" Dad says. The men go into some long conversation about the football season—which doesn't even start for another month. I rush over to Maggie. She and Callie sweep me into a three-way hug.

"Daija, you really looked amazing," says Maggie.

"Together, you guys looked like a beautiful painting come to life," says Callie.

"Thank you, guys." *Dang!* I try not to show it, but I think I'm tearing up a little.

I hear Dad say to Mr. West, "I'll be right back."

"Where's your stepmom and the boys?" Callie asks.

"Her mother is in the hospital. She kept the boys with her," I say. I feel bad about her mother. I know they're close. Speaking of mothers, Kiki appears at my side looking devilish.

"Are you happy now?" she says.

"Very!" I reply. I turn around, looking back at Mr. West. "I wonder where Dad went."

Mr. West, wearing shorts and sweat socks with a headband around his forehead, is just too funny-looking.

Maggie catches me staring at him and says, "No, girl, don't say it. I'm begging you." Both Callie and I stifle giggles. I turn all the way around again, looking for Dad. Two little girls from camp come up to me.

"You look really pretty," says one.

The other says, "And you dance pretty, too. I wish I was a ballerina girl." It's hard to explain the type of pride mixed with honor I feel going through me.

I thank the little girls and hug them. Their mother is standing a few feet back. She smiles. "They wanted to meet you," she says. "I guess I know who's going to be taking her kids to dance class in the fall."

We all laugh. Then Callie says, "Hey, Daija, there's your dad."

I turn just as my father reaches me. He is carrying the biggest bouquet of roses I've ever seen. Yellow and white, with huge sprays of baby's breath tucked between the stems.

"To my beautiful dancing girl," he says. "I may not always be here as often as I'd like, but you are never far from my mind. Thank you for letting me be a part of your day."

When he hands the huge batch of flowers to me, I can't hold back. The tears rush down my cheeks.

"Oh, *Daaad*!" I say, crying into the floral tissue paper. Both he and Mom are laughing and patting my back.

Through my blurred vision, I see Mr. West as he says, "Um, Callie, Maggie, I didn't get you guys a garden full of roses, but I have some gum in the car."

Maggie replies, "Daddy, *I'll* give *you* flowers if you'll just go home and put on some pants!"

That snaps me out of the tears as we all laugh.

It's official. This is the greatest night of my life, so far. I look over at Kiki, and she looks misty-eyed, too.

I feel a peace and joy inside myself that I instantly realize has been missing. I guess I got so into the Braid Girls for more than the money—it was the winning part. Feeling like I'd accomplished something important.

That need got in the way of common sense and almost cost me my best friend. I have to make sure never to let that happen again.

Kiki and my father are talking, actually talking, without yelling or storming off. I hope they can have more conversations like that. I hope the next time, my stepmom can make it, too.

Looking at Mr. West in his ridiculous sweat socks and headband, I laugh to myself. I still think Maggie is pretty dang lucky. Her family is close to perfect. Then again, no one is *perfect*, especially not my family. Perfect or not, they are mine, and I love them.

CHAPTER 25

Callie

A light of happiness moves through me like sunshine. I can't believe I just did a dance with my own dad.

It feels great.

I'm tired, though. Not just from dancing and all the practice Dad and I've been doing, but from working out with Daija, too. I find a chair and stretch, taking in some deep breaths. I make up my own chant:

I'm in charge of my emotions.

These days, I've been feeling a little more in

control. I'm finding that lately, since me and my dad spoke, I don't feel like I'm being forced to live by a certain philosophy to honor my mom.

She only wanted me to be happy in life.

I've moved to a wooden chair beside the folding tables. I'm now in my lotus position, letting the sun warm my hair and each inch of skin on my cheeks, forehead, and neck. I can see Maggie pretending to be super horrified that Dad is still busting out the old dance moves. Secretly, though, I know she feels proud to have him here, too.

I keep repeating my chant, eyes closed. At some point a shadow brushes away the sun and moves across my face. At first, I don't bother opening my eyes. Then I feel a tap on my wrist.

"Hey," a voice says, "they're playing your song." Maggie is smiling, holding out her hand. Daija is right beside her.

Then I realize it's "Atlantis" by Anais.

We all start singing, even Tina and our dad. Singing and laughing about how I've listened to the song so much, everybody knows it.

Five weeks earlier, when I got here, I felt like Anais was the only person in the world who understood me. Now I know better.

Still, it's a great song.

And a great song deserves to be sung!

CHAPTER 26

The Braid Girls

Walking out of the park later, Callie, Daija, and Maggie are side by side.

"Girls, you know school will be starting in no time," says Maggie. "We're going to need to work on our marketing if we want to build our brand for the school crowd."

The girls are all blabbering about different things—but they're doing it together.

"That bracelet is so pretty," Daija says, grabbing Maggie's arm. "Where'd you get it?" Maggie looks at Callie and smiles.

"From my sister."

Daija says, "We could sell them and make more money."

"I hope Keith likes it," mutters Maggie, still admiring her wrist. "Do you think I look good in bracelets?"

Callie stands in her sun salutation pose chanting, "Love is power. Love is power. Love is power."

Daija looks from Maggie to Callie. "Don't make me have to remind either one of you who was here first—ME! I'm a sister, too!" she insists.

Both sisters snap off perfect salutes.

"*Goodness!*" says Daija. The three walk along, each in her own joy bubble. Daija says, "My father invited the three of us to come over to his house and swim next weekend. I still really want to get into the fall showcase, but if I don't, maybe it's not the end of the world."

"Not the end of the world, eh?" Maggie says. "Wow."

"Shut up, Maggie!" Daija says, laughing and shoving her.

A voice shouts: "Turn around!"

It's Keith, with his camera. He grins, blushing when he looks at Maggie. The two of them are as cute as puppies.

He jogs closer and aims his camera.

"Say 'Braid Girls!'" he says.

And they do.

Acknowledgments

Every book requires a village to bring it to life. I would like to acknowledge all the braiders who allowed me to pick their brains as they threaded magic into my hair. Also, I want to thank my agent, Laurie Liss, for her unyielding support, and my family at Little, Brown Books for Young Readers.

Don't miss Sherri Winston's amazing books.

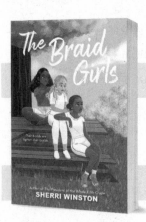

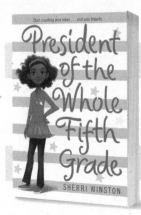

STORIES ABOUT FRIENDSHIP, GROWING UP, AND FINDING YOURSELF!

 LITTLE, BROWN AND COMPANY
BOOKS FOR YOUNG READERS

LBYR.co